LOV E
in an
E XPANDING
UNIVE RS E

E

LOV E
in an
XPANDI NG
U NIVE RS E

n
e RIVERS PRESS
w MSUM

stories by
Ron Rindo

The publication of *Love in an Expanding Universe* is made possible by the generous support of the Jerome Foundation. Additional support has been provided by the McKnight Foundation and other contributing members.

For academic permission please contact Frederick T. Courtright at 570-839-7477 or permdude@eclipse.net. For all other permissions, contact The Copyright Clearance Center at 978-750-8400 or info@copyright.com.

New Rivers Press is a nonprofit literary press associated with Minnesota State University Moorhead.

Wayne Gudmundson, Director
Alan Davis, Senior Editor
Thom Tammaro, Poetry Editor
Donna Carlson, Managing Editor
     Honors Apprentice: Rosanne Pfenning
     Love in an Expanding Universe book team: Samantha Miller, Kurt Olerud
     Editorial interns: Fauntel DeShayes, Tessa Dietz, Kacy Friddle, Diana
          Goble, Jill Haugen, Amber Langford, Jens Larson,
          Samantha Miller, Kurt Olerud, Tamera Parrish, Heather
          Steinmann, Melissa Sumas, Abbey Thompsen.
     Design interns: Katie Elenberger, Allison Garske, Amanda Ketterling,
          Jocie Salveson, Lindsay Staber, Amy Wilcox.
     Communications Coordinator: Gerri Stowman; Teresa Schafer
     Literary Festival Coordinator: Jill Haugen
     Fundraising Coordinator: Jens Larson
     Web Site Coordinator: Conor Shenk
Marlane Sanderson; Deb Hval, Business Manager
Allen Sheets, Design Manager
Nancy E. Hanson, Events Manager
Liz Conmey, Marketing Manager

Printed in the United States of America.

Many Voices Project Number 106

New Rivers Press
c/o MSUM
1104 7th Avenue South
Moorhead, MN 56563
www.newriverspress.com

for Jenna

Contents

The Book of Love is long and boring
And written very long ago.
It's full of flowers and heart-shaped boxes
And things we're all too young to know.

Stephen Merritt
"The Book of Love"
The Magnetic Fields, 69 Love Songs

C

Crop Dusting

Karen lives out in the country now in a butter-yellow house with her new husband and three children, his two girls from a previous marriage, who stay with them every other weekend, and the baby boy they just had together. The house is a two-story colonial set back in the woods, with a big country porch out front and a lawn as green and manicured as a golf course.

Across the road are eighty rolling acres planted with field corn. I know it's not sweet corn because this field never gets sprayed. In late summer the Delmonte company, which rents a lot of the farmland around here, hires crop dusters to spray pesticides on its sweet corn to kill the corn borers. The pilots work in the gray light of early dawn when the air is still, buzzing so close to the corn in their yellow planes that their wings nearly brush the pollen off the tassels. When they get to the end of a field and reach the hedgerow, it looks as if someone above them pulls a string, and they turn straight up and disappear over the trees. You can hear the whine of their engines grow faint, then louder, as they circle back for another pass. I imagine those pilots are having a hell of a time, flying so fast and so close to the ground. Watching them almost makes you forget about every bad thing that's ever happened to you.

I work second shift, two-thirty to eleven, at a place that makes office furniture, and sometimes if I stop at Kwik Trip to grab a bag of chips for supper I don't even get to the cornfield until after midnight. I pull off County Road M about a half-mile from Karen's house, and I follow the dirt lane between the corn and a tangled hedgerow of raspberry canes and box elder trees until it makes a little bend and my truck can no longer be seen. And then I walk between the rows of corn, mashing clods of dirt beneath my boots, smelling the syrupy juice in each stalk, moths fluttering around my head. The thick leaves and sticky silks brush against the sleeves of my flannel shirt. I find the spot maybe nine or ten rows in, straight across the road from her house, and I spread out my tarp and my sleeping bag. Now that it's early August, the corn is over eight feet tall, but on a clear night, I can look up and see every star in the sky. As often as I come to the cornfield, each time I lay down, I have this strange feeling, like I can't quite believe I'm really there. Sometimes in life you find yourself in surprising places. This is what my therapist says, though I've never told him where I spend my nights.

Once in a while, Karen will still be awake when I get there. She'll be reading a novel with the light on, lying in a t-shirt next to Paul, her new husband. She always reads when she has trouble falling asleep. I like to think that sometimes she can't sleep because she's thinking about me.

I set my watch alarm for five a.m., close my eyes, and try to sleep. You'd think that midnight in the country would be all quiet and peaceful, but that's not the case. The dark is alive with things: bats, opossums, coyotes, raccoons, owls, rabbits, weasels, skunks, deer. Folks get up in the morning and go to work, or on the weekends they cut and fertilize their lawns, weed their flowerbeds, and they think they have the whole world to themselves. But they don't. They share it with things few people ever see.

One night thousands of June bugs crawled up out of the ground and swarmed in the air, big as flying grapes and as hard as hailstones. And sometimes so many moths hover around Karen's porch lights that they look like a snowstorm. Some of the moths look as large as sparrows. But the true rulers of the night are mosquitoes. The music of the collected beating of their wings is like the song of the sirens, luring the unsuspecting traveler into misery.

Guy I know at work says Wisconsin mosquitoes get so big they can stand flat-footed and hump a chicken. Says he's heard of farmers losing livestock. In a single night a million mosquitoes can draw all the blood and flesh right through a cow's Guernsey hide, like a kid sucking a milkshake through a straw. Reports farmers finding just the skin and bones out in the morning pasture, like clothes someone just took off and dropped, sticks left in the pockets. Says if he ever caught his wife in bed with another man, he'd tie that man naked to a chair out in a swampy Wisconsin field, let the mosquitoes go at him all night. Slather honey on his dick for good measure.

Hell, I know it's not right, what I'm doing. But I can't help it. I'm not a bad person. Up until my divorce from Karen I had never even set foot inside a courthouse or had any contact with the police whatsoever. I take that back. One time I did get stopped for speeding. I had our boy in the car with me, six years old then, blood pouring from his pulpy lips. The school nurse called me at work and I picked him up and headed for the hospital, driving like a maniac, his blood all over my shirt. I got pulled over, but that cop took one look at my boy—Charlie was his name—bleeding from the mouth, and it was like in the movies. I said, He got hit by a baseball bat at school. And the cop just said, Follow me. He took off with his lights flashing, and he led us to the hospital emergency room. Charlie'd had two of his baby teeth knocked out and needed seven stitches in his lip, but he forgot all about it while we were following that cop car doing seventy miles per hour. And not on the freeway, either.

What I'm trying to say is, I'm someone who obeys the law. I'm a good person. But things aren't right for me. I tell myself, maybe I'm not breaking any laws anyway, you know? No law against still being so in love with someone you sit all night in a cornfield watching her house in case a fire would start or something, so you could rush in and save her. Is there a law against that kind of love?

✖   ✖   ✖   ✖   ✖

It's not as if my whole life is out there with the owls and moths. Every Sunday afternoon I visit my father at the nursing home. Dad's seventy-three. He's got inoperable bone cancer and diabetes and some form of dementia, maybe Alzheimer's, maybe not, they don't know. The cancer has sprawled throughout his body, into his liver, his kidneys, his lungs. They didn't expect him to live past Christmas, but he surprised them. He's confused, though. Even in his most lucid moments, he thinks I'm married to some woman named Beretta, which is an Italian brand of shotgun he used to hunt pheasants with. I've never told him that Karen and I got divorced. He also seems to have forgotten that Charlie is dead.

This Sunday I wander in and he's sleeping on his back, the TV tuned to some football pregame show. His hair is white and long, down to his shoulders now, since he won't let anyone cut it. He's got tufts of hair growing out of each nostril and inside his ears, and his eyebrows are so long you could braid them. He looks like an old, skinny tree being taken over by moss. I set down the shoebox of Legos I brought him, and I look at the house he made with the last box, assembled on the table next to his bed. It's the same house he always makes, the three-bedroom ranch house I grew up in, red brick with a black roof. Up until Mom's cancer, which came when Dad was already starting to forget the way home from the grocery store, he had spent every day of his life in that house. He can't remember what he had for breakfast, but every time I bring him a new box of Legos, he builds that house, with every detail exactly right, including the missing bricks up on the chimney, where it was hit by lightning in 1989. Sometimes he'll look at it and start crying, but when I ask him why he's sad, he just shakes his head and says he doesn't know.

I turn off the TV, and the sudden quiet wakes him up.

"Who's there?" he shouts, opening his eyes.

"It's just me, Dad," I tell him. I notice they've still got him strapped to the bed. One afternoon a month ago he pulled out his IV and disappeared. Three hours later they found him asleep in the sporting goods aisle at Wal-Mart, the pockets of his bathrobe filled with ping-pong balls. I open the buckles and loosen the straps.

"You," he says, staring at me. "Who the hell are you?"

"Larry," I tell him. "Your son."

"Since when?"

"Since thirty-seven years ago," I say.

He stares at me, confused. Suddenly, he puts his arms over his head like he's a referee signaling a touchdown. "Guess what!" he says, excitedly.

"What?"

"I've been elected the governor of South Dakota!"

"You're kidding!" I say.

"No," he says, "it's true."

This makes me smile. "That's a pretty good trick, Dad, especially since we live in Wisconsin."

"I know!" he says. "It's a miracle!"

I know better than to argue with him. If I ever disagree with him, he gets furious. He screams himself hoarse, flails around in his bed.

"What's your agenda as governor?" I ask.

"What the Christ is agenda?"

"Your plan," I say. "You know, what you want to accomplish."

He nods and holds up an index finger. "My plan," he says. He leans toward me and motions with his hand to get closer, so he can whisper in my ear. But he speaks in his regular voice. "I'm going to change the name so it ends in a consonant. I hate states that end in vowels. It makes them sound fruity." I laugh but he points a finger at me. "I'm serious," he says.

"So what are you going to call it, Dad? South Dakot?"

He shakes his head. "I don't know." He reaches across his bed to grab a puzzle of the United States that he keeps on the nightstand. Ever since the onset of his dementia, he's been fascinated with maps. He points. "Look at this! You can't drive all the way across without passing through a state that ends in a vowel. Did you know that? You get started in Oregon or Washington, okay, fine, but then what happens? You hit Montana or Idaho. Or you hit California or Colorado or Arizona or New Mexico. Go north and you hit Canada!" He shakes his head in astonishment, as if a country that ends in a vowel is almost too much to endure. "And even if you some-how manage it, and I don't know how the Christ you would, you still face the Dakotas, or Iowa, or Nebraska. You're fucked. It can't be done." He looks angry.

"I guess not."

"Whose idea was it to give all these states names that end in vowels?"

"I don't know."

"Fucking Republicans," he says. He takes a deep breath and throws the puzzle off the side of his bed. The pieces scatter on the floor.

His chin drops to his chest. I kneel, pile the pieces on the puzzle, and put it on his nightstand. Then I stand up and turn the TV back on. I adjust the volume so we can hear it if we want to, but not so loud that we can't talk. Dad looks up at me again. "How's Beretta?" he asks.

"She's doing fine, Dad."

"She's got a nice ass," he says.

I nod at him. "Yes she does."

"Tight as a peach," he says.

I nod at him and smile.

"You should bring her in some time."

"I should."

"What about your boy? What the Christ is his name?"

"Charlie."

"Why the hell don't you ever bring him by to see me?"

"I should do that," I say.

"Why the Christ not?" He scratches his head. Then he looks distressed, frightened, even. "Don't ever bring him here," he says. There is panic in his voice. "Do you hear me?"

"Okay."

Tears pool in his eyes. He looks around the room furtively, as if there is some evil lurking there. "Oh Christ, no. Don't bring him."

"Okay, Dad," I say. "I won't." I pat him on the arm, hold his hand for awhile to calm him. I point to the box of Legos sitting on the floor. "I brought you some more Legos," I tell him. "I like the house you made with the last box."

He nods. Like always, I'll take this house back to my apartment with me and disassemble it, then I'll put the pieces in a box and bring them back the next week. Dad stares down at his hands and moves his mouth like he's chewing gum.

"Why don't we watch some football?" I say. "The Packers play the Vikings today. Should be a good one."

He nods and wipes his eyes with his fingers the way a child might. "Oh Christ, the Vikings," he says. "They're from Minnesota."

I nod.

"I hate that state," he says.

✖   ✖   ✖   ✖   ✖

Love is a many splendored thing. Love means never having to say you're sorry. Love is all you need. Love love love love love love love. I'm sick of hearing about it. Love is a disease. It's an addiction. They should have Lovers Anonymous meetings and everyone should go. You could sit there in a circle and say, "My name's Larry and I'm in love and it's ruining my life," and everyone around you would smile like imbeciles and nod and say, "Hi Larry!"

I mean, think about what you read in the paper! Some loser spends all his savings to buy his girlfriend a diamond the size of a sugar cube. He'd crawl through fire for this girl, right, he's so crazy for her. But then a week later or a month later or a year later, it doesn't matter, she dumps him. The next thing you know he's at her house with a shotgun and he says if I can't have you, nobody can have you. He blows a hole the size of a dinner plate through her chest and then sticks the gun in his mouth, and the detectives are picking pieces of his skull out of the ceiling tiles. You tell me: how much splendor is there in that?

Karen and I have been divorced over a year, but I *still* can't sleep at home in my own bed, not well, not through the night. All those memories start marching through my brain like termites, and I can't take it. I feel hollowed out inside. I start to sweat and my hands start to shake. And believe me, it doesn't help when a therapist tells you this is all normal, when he says, "sometimes life takes you to surprising places that we're not quite prepared to visit," like divorce is a fucking trip to Disneyland. He says I have anger issues. He says I have guilt issues. He says grieving a divorce is like grieving a death. At a hundred and twenty-five bucks an hour, you'd think he could tell me something I don't already know.

The first time I went out to Karen's house, it was February, cold as hell, snow flying everywhere. I think I just cracked, or something. I panicked. I got in my truck and drove out there, about three in the morning, no idea of what I was doing, really, or why. I was not coherent. I had a bottle of beer between my legs. I had a joint burning in the ashtray. One more thing: I had a gun in the truck, a deer rifle in a case behind the seat, but that didn't mean anything. I had no clear intentions. I was crazy. I was really just—crazy.

When I got close to her house, I turned my lights off and sort of glided in quietly through the snow. I drove by. The whole house was dark except for the glow of nightlights in the children's rooms. I kept driving past her house in the dark, back and forth, over and over and over. It made my heart slow down.

A couple nights later I drove out there again. Next night the same thing, only I parked my truck on the side of the road, far enough away so I wouldn't be seen, but close enough where I could see her house through the trees. I just sat there and looked at the house. It made me feel safe. That's how it all started. Couple nights a week in the winter, maybe three or four nights a week in the spring. As the weather warmed it got to be even more often. Only now I can't sleep anyplace else except in this cornfield across from her house. Sometimes it's all I can think about. I'm at work and it's ten o'clock and I'm thinking, only two more hours.

To feel better about myself I imagine I'm a guardian angel or a god with a small g, not a manipulating God, but a god who mostly watches.

Sometimes, though, I do a little more. Like in May, on the one-year anniversary of our divorce, a few weeks after Karen had her baby, I snuck down the road—staying low because the corn had just sprouted, so if I wasn't in the woods I had no place to hide—and I poured a full envelope of Morning Glory seeds in the dirt under her mailbox. In the picture on the envelope the flowers looked like little blue trumpets. It made me think of Charlie being born, of seeing him come out of her body all wrinkled and wet and alive. Now those green morning glory vines have covered the post and the paper box and the mail box, trailing their tangled vines and beautiful blue flowers everywhere.

✖ ✖ ✖ ✖ ✖

Sometimes when I visit my father he thinks he's someone else. He thinks he's the commissioner of baseball or the mayor of New York. Sometimes he thinks people outside of his window are trying to assassinate him. He'll scream that I have to close the curtains. I'll look out the window and I'll see an old woman walking her dog, and he'll say, "Old woman, my ass! That's a disguise. And that's no dog, either. You must be blind to think that's an actual dog."

If I'm lucky I'll be able to change the subject. I'll talk about sports and he'll get distracted enough to forget about the imagined threats on his life, or the responsibilities of his imaginary office.

Though we're at opposite ends of it, my father and I have something in common. We're like the two heads of the king of hearts, joined at the torso. What you have when you are too strongly tied to your past is no better than when you have no reliable connection there at all. Can't remember, can't forget, it's misery either way.

✖ ✖ ✖ ✖ ✖

In mid-July, early on a Saturday morning, maybe 1 a.m., I brought a six-pack out to the cornfield with me, and I fell asleep and forgot to set my watch alarm. I awoke to sunshine, nearly eight o'clock in the morning, my head heavy as a watermelon. I heard a door slam. I heard windows sliding open. I sat up, startled, and I saw Karen on the front porch in a rocking chair, breast-feeding her baby. The corn was about four feet high. The sun bright. Maybe I could have crawled the half-mile or so through the corn to my truck, but the risk seemed too great. And so I watched her there, sitting in blue jeans, barefoot, her t-shirt pulled up over a breast.

The baby was two months old. I didn't even know his name. I only know it was a boy because they'd had a stork sign, "IT'S A BOY!" on the front door for a few days. Watching her with that baby reminded me of watching her breast-feed Charlie, watching that hungry little guy pull her dark nipple deep into his mouth, listening to him swallow.

Later that morning things almost unraveled. Paul was outside with one of his daughters. She's maybe six years old, brown hair, a pretty little girl. She wore a purple helmet and sat on a little white bicycle with training wheels, and Paul was pushing her up and down their gravel driveway. Eventually she started riding on her own, big smile on her face, and he was clapping for her. Then the phone rang. Karen went inside, and a little while later she poked her head out the door and called Paul. He went inside, too. The little girl kept riding that bicycle. When she came to the end of the driveway she stopped. She looked at the cornfield, and I swear, it seemed as if she were looking right at me. I was crouched down on my belly, trapped there. Then she seemed to get distracted, and she pedaled her bicycle right out onto the road, marveling at the smooth pull of her tires on the blacktop.

I heard a dump truck hauling gravel, a big one, heard it coming around the corner, downshifting, burning oil, maybe two hundred yards from where this little girl was pedaling her bike. She stared straight down at the road, concentrating on her balance, oblivious to everything around her. The noise of the approaching truck grew louder. I decided then it didn't matter who knew or who saw me, but I wasn't going to let that little girl get hit by that truck on her bicycle. I got up to my knees and was squatting on my feet, ready to run out of the field, and then Paul appeared, right there next to her, and he calmly pushed her bicycle back to the driveway.

✖   ✖   ✖   ✖   ✖

Sunday when I arrive at the nursing home, Dad is in trouble. He's thrashing against the straps holding him down, and two nurses are leaning over his bed, trying to calm him. He is frightened of something, I can tell that much. The food from his lunch tray is scattered across the bed and on the floor.

"Dad," I say, rushing in to help. "Calm down."

He shouts something incomprehensible, an animal sound. He's been crying. His eyes are bloodshot and his red cheeks shine. He's soiled himself, too. The smell is awful.

One of the nurses says, "He thought the Jell-O was poison."

"It is." She frowns at me. "Is he getting bad?" I ask.

She nods at me. "He was up most of the night."

"How bad?" I ask.

She smiles sympathetically and shrugs.

Within a minute or so Dad calms down. He lies back and closes his eyes. I bend down and begin picking his food from the floor. The Jell-O squares, red and green, look like little colored dice.

"We just have to change his diaper and we'll be done," the nurse says. She is a chunky woman with a kind, calm face.

Eventually they get him cleaned up. He stares at the ceiling and moves his mouth like he's sucking on a lozenge. Then he notices I'm sitting there and he turns toward me. His eyes are vacant. He speaks a few, incomprehensible sentences, then closes his eyes again.

"Shhhh, Dad," I say. I run a hand over his forehead, gently, and then down his hair. His body smells sour. "It's all right, " I tell him, in a soft voice. "Everything is all right." I don't know if he is even going to last the night. He opens his eyes.

He blinks. "Hurts," he says.

"I know," I tell him. I kiss him once on the forehead. Morphine drips from a clear, plastic bag through a tube and into his hand.

I go out to the desk and ask the nurses what they think, and they both say it's so hard to tell, that it could be any time, a matter of hours or a matter of days. I stay until almost two in the morning, sitting with him, holding his hand.

I come back every day after that, sit with him, rub my hand over his hot forehead. He's stopped eating and the morphine keeps him asleep most of the time. Back when he still had moments of lucidity he had signed papers forbidding the use of a respirator or a g-tube to keep him alive.

After four long days of this, his condition has changed little. Just after midnight, the night nurse pokes her head in and says, "Go home, get some rest. I'll call you if there's any change." And so I make the hour and ten-minute drive to Karen's house, roll out my sleeping bag, try to sleep.

My father hangs on for over a week, sleeping and moaning, moaning and sleeping. His skin is yellowed and tight over his bones. The urine in his catheter bag is the color of coffee. I sit with him, holding the drying, age-spotted claw of his left hand. One of the nurses comes in and says, "Sometimes the brain and body quit working, but the heart won't give up. It doesn't know any better." She touches my back softly. "It's something, isn't it?"

"It's something," I say.

I think about my father's hatred of states that end in vowels. This makes me smile. I check his puzzle of the United States to see if it is possible to drive from one coast to the other without encountering such a state, and I discover that he's right. It's impossible. I begin to run the words of my life through my head, sorting those that end in consonants—the good ones—from those that end in vowels. The vowel list is a chronicle of loss: love, wife, intimacy, marriage, Charlie, adultery, divorce, hate, chemotherapy, nursing home, morphine, all those *Y*s and silent *E*s stacking up like the cars in a train wreck.

I fall asleep with my head on the railing of his bed. After midnight, one of the nurses wakes me. "If there's any change, we'll call you," she says.

I head for the cornfield.

In the early morning, before sunrise, I return to my apartment. When I get there, the light on my answering machine is blinking. The first two messages are from the night nurse, telling me that my father is not doing well, that his breathing has grown labored. The last one tells me that it's four-thirty in the morning, and my father has died.

"He waited until you were gone," the morning nurse tells me, when I call. "We see that a lot."

"He waited," I ask, blankly.

"Well yes," she said. "He did."

✳   ✳   ✳   ✳   ✳

Karen and I met in college, did all those college things together— smoked dope, went out and partied, learned what our bodies could do in the back seat of a car, in the twin bed of a dorm room, on a blanket at the beach. Karen was a business major and I majored in English. She used to joke, with her business-school sense of superiority, that my English major was good preparation for a career as a bartender or a waiter. I'd say in response: Who would you rather marry, a man who can balance his checkbook right down to the penny or a man who will write you love poems in soap on the bathroom mirror?

When Charlie was born, I fell so in love with him I used to take a chair into his room to watch him sleep. My God. What a beautiful thing a young child is! I'd sit for hours. Kids are a lot of work, sure, but what you don't expect is the way you're going to love them, the way they're going to curl up in the chambers of your heart and feed you, and hold you hostage.

When Charlie was seven, almost two years ago now, he was walking to school alone. It was a cool fall morning, October 6th. Some high school kid showing off for his girlfriend in a Volkswagen Jetta came howling down the street, and Charlie must have been daydreaming or something and he stepped out from between two parked cars.

When I heard the sirens I ran all seven blocks down to the school. I didn't even put shoes on. I ran out in my socks and bathrobe and the whole way I was thinking what are the odds, you know? It couldn't be about Charlie. It couldn't be. When I got to where the police cars were parked, their lights throbbing, I saw the paramedics swarming over his body like hornets. I used someone's cell phone to call Karen at work. One of Charlie's shoes, a Power Rangers tennis shoe with two Velcro straps, was sitting twenty feet away on the road.

I didn't know it then, but Charlie had become the glue that was holding me and Karen together those seven years. And when he was gone, the house went quiet, and our lives slipped apart. She blamed me for Charlie's death, and she was right. I was to blame. What man is so tired he can't walk his own kid to school every day if he's home in the mornings? What man sends his seven-year-old son walking alone to school so he can drink his coffee and read the morning paper?

Karen started working later and later. We stopped talking. In our despair, our relationship traveled backwards. We became strangers again. By the time I accepted that we should try counseling, she was already sleeping with Paul.

⁕ ⁕ ⁕ ⁕ ⁕

My father's funeral has the allure of a celebration. The visitation is from six until eight, with the memorial service to follow. A lot of people show up, a lot more than I had anticipated. My therapist arrives and stays for a while, which is a little weird. Some of the guys from work come in, and I appreciate that. They mill around uncomfortably in the ties they bought just for the occasion and talk about sports, or about some of the women who work at the factory. A lot of mom and dad's friends show up from the old neighborhood, people I haven't seen for ten or fifteen years, some of them wobbling on canes, happy to have the chance to go out dressed in their Sunday suits and skirts. They are boisterous and even jovial, some of them, shouting and winking and telling stories about my father that make all of them laugh out loud. They tell of the time Dad started the charcoal in his barbecue grill with gasoline and in the process lit the eaves of his house on fire. They talk about the time he over-fertilized the lawn and turned it all brown. They laugh and slap my back.

Then Karen and Paul come in. I look up at the door and they're there, and I feel as if I'm hallucinating. I know the funeral director had placed my father's obituary in the paper, but you never think people actually read the thing and follow through. Karen is wearing a black skirt and a dark blue blouse, and her curly hair is combed long and straight, down to her shoulders. Paul wears a gray suit and lavender tie. They file past the memorial table, where there are about a dozen pictures of my father propped up in frames, surrounded by flowers, with the urn holding his ashes propped in the middle of the table like the turkey on Thanksgiving. They smile and examine the pictures, with Karen lifting a few of the frames for a closer look. Then they approach me calmly, their faces serious and peaceful.

Karen walks straight through my extended hand and hugs me. "Larry, I'm so sorry," she says. She rises up on her toes, as she always did. I have not touched her for so long, she feels new to me. I encircle her back with my arms, feel her hair against my chin, her breasts against my chest, smell her perfume. She leans back, takes both of my hands in hers, looks up into my face.

I smile and nod at her. I feel as if I'm in shock, but I maintain my composure. "Thank you," I say. She is wearing dark lipstick and mascara. She has small diamonds in her pierced ears.

Paul and I meet eyes. He is a partner at the same accounting firm where Karen works. He offers a sympathetic wince, then reaches out awkwardly to touch my arm. "I'm sorry for your loss," he says. Karen is still holding my hands.

Paul nods at me. He kisses Karen on the back of the head and then moves away, walks toward a row of chairs, and sits down.

"You look well," Karen says, letting my hands go.

"I feel like crap," I say.

"That's understandable, under the circumstances."

We stand together and stare at the floor, an awkward silence sprouting in the space between us.

"Congratulations on your new baby, by the way," I tell her.

"Thank you," she says. "His name is Andrew. Andrew Charles."

Charles was my father's name. Charles was Charlie's name. It seems as if my knees might buckle. The room suddenly feels hot. Karen senses my shock and reaches out to put her hand on my arm. I am unable to speak.

Karen says, "I didn't think you'd mind. It's not like I've left everything behind, Larry."

I nod. I am struggling to keep from crying. She takes my arm gently by the elbow and leads me toward the wall, where we are away from all of the others.

She smiles. "You used to drive past my house, didn't you," she says. "In the winter. When I was pregnant with Andy. Sometimes I couldn't sleep, and I would just sit in a rocking chair out on the landing, looking out the windows at the snow, thinking about Charlie. Sometimes I would just sit there, crying. And then one night I saw you. I didn't think it was you at first, but when you went past again, and then again the next night, I knew."

I nod.

She rolls her eyes. "Paul wanted to call the police." She takes a deep breath, sighs, looks away. "I know you won't believe this, but it was all just as hard for me as it was for you, Larry. All of it. Just as hard."

"It's been hard for me," I say, nodding, the tears starting to come.

She squeezes my shoulder with her hand. "I know. It's so hard. What part of the past to keep? What part to let go? How to remember? I had to see someone for awhile, to get through it."

"A shrink?"

"A therapist, yes. She said to try to think of your life as a fishing boat, with nets strung out behind it. You try to trap all that is good in your nets, all that you need to keep, and then let what is harmful or hurtful flow through so you can continue moving forward."

"If I trolled for tuna I'd catch a net full of dolphins. Greenpeace would be all over my ass."

"What are you talking about?"

"It's a joke," I tell her.

She smiles.

"I don't know how to move forward," I say.

"It takes time," she says. "That's a cliché, I know. But it's true."

"I miss Charlie," I say. "I miss everything."

She gives me a sad, pathetic look. "I miss Charlie, too," she says.

Someone clears his throat. I look up. The funeral director is asking people to move toward the chapel. Everyone flows slowly toward rows of metal folding chairs arranged on each side of a center aisle, in front of the podium. The funeral director stands stiffly in his dark suit, preparing to lead my father's memorial service. Karen squeezes my hand and turns to join her husband. I move woodenly toward my seat of honor in the front row.

When the memorial service is ended, I turn around, but Karen and Paul are already gone.

⋇   ⋇   ⋇   ⋇   ⋇

I am the last one to leave the funeral home. I sign all the papers, shake hands with the director, who expresses his sympathy yet again for the loss of my father. The silver urn holding Dad's ashes is engraved with trees and birds of paradise. It has a cover like one you'd find on an expensive cookie jar, and it is surprisingly heavy—perhaps the weight of a large sack of flour you'd buy at the grocery store.

It's after ten o'clock when I start my truck, pull out of the now empty parking lot. Even diluted by the lights of the city, the moon is full and bright. I stop at a diner for coffee, sit alone, empty the first cup and half of the second. My waitress has the hyperactive friendliness of someone juiced on caffeine and in love with a new boyfriend. She is wearing a boy's class ring on a piece of yarn around her neck. I notice her eyes as she pours my second cup. They fall on the urn. I have brought my father's ashes into the diner with me. They rest next to me on the padded bench seat.

"Is that a trophy?" she asks, happily. "Did you win something?"

This makes me smile. "No," I tell her. I shake my head. "It's not a trophy."

"Oh," she says, her smile dropping. "It looks like a trophy."

It's after eleven when I pay my bill, carry the urn back to my truck. I think about going home, but I know that I really don't intend to go there. I turn the opposite direction, toward Karen's house. It's a 45-minute drive.

I've got Dad's ashes on my lap, the bottom of the urn balanced between my legs on the seat. Just out of town, a family of raccoons crosses the road and I slow down to avoid hitting them. They scramble in my headlight beams and disappear in the tall grass growing along the shoulder.

Twenty minutes go by, and up ahead, something catches my eye. Fireflies. Not the usual handful of flickering tails, but whole patches of flashing light, in small groups at first, and then completely covering the sky, thousands of them. When I reach them with my truck, I hear the ticking of their bodies as they strike my windshield and coalesce in an eerie, green-glowing fuzz. There are so many I have to turn on my windshield wipers, pump washer fluid, just so I can see where I'm going. It's like a meteor shower. They are everywhere—glowing like a carpet of fire on the road, over the road, and up in the trees. When I can no longer see, I pull over, stop, get out of my truck and walk into them. They land on me freely, hover against my face, my lips, my ears. When I look back, the windshield, hood, and front grill are glowing with the fire of their bodies. I sit down right in the grass and watch them, awestruck.

Then almost as quickly, most of them are gone. They go dark. The breeze kicks up and they either fly away or stop glowing.

I get back in my truck and drive on.

When I get about a mile down the road from Karen's, I see something that almost makes me panic. Ahead, where the cornfield should be, all I see is bright light and open sky. At first, I think maybe it's just fireflies again, lighting the whole field, or maybe the moon, but I can't

tell for sure. I grip the steering wheel tightly. I swallow. When I reach
the field, the blood rushes to my head, and I can feel my stomach tight-
en. The field has been harvested. Where days before there had been
eighty acres of lush field corn, all that remains are the jointed stumps
of the severed corn stalks, row upon endless row. I slow to a stop,
turn up the dirt lane I have entered so many times. My headlights cut
across the open field and in the distance I see the glowing eyes of twenty or thirty deer, browsing for spilled corn. I turn off my lights and cut
the engine. In my stomach, I can feel the throbbing of my pulse. I put
my hands on my father's urn and blink back tears. The moon is so
bright, my truck casts a shadow.

"Dad," I say. I look down at the urn. I am talking to ashes. "Karen
and I are divorced, Dad, and Charlie is dead. He was hit by a car."

I look out over the field. With the corn gone, I feel exposed.
Everything looks different. I turn the key of my truck and start the
engine. By mistake, I shift into forward instead of reverse, but when
I hit the gas and roll up into the harvested field, I suddenly decide to
keep going. What the hell, I think. Why not? The truck rolls and rocks
gently through the small valleys and over the clods of dirt. I push on
the gas, turn on the headlights, and head up the hill, toward the deer.
I accelerate as I reach them, and I smile as they scatter across the field
like ghosts, some of then bounding left, some right, their white tails
high, like sails. When I reach the top of the hill, I stop. The engine
idles. I roll down my window. Even in the darkness, I can see for miles.
Far across the field, a cloud of fireflies appears.

I look down at the urn between my legs. I remove the cover, put
a hand inside, feel the ashes, like cool water, against my fingers.
With both hands, I lift the urn to the open window, tip it to its side until some of the ash begins to spill out. With my left arm, I hold it there.

I shift into gear. Then I punch the gas and drive as fast as I can.

Mi

d dleman

For Fred, Large-hearted Boy

When my wife Julia and I pulled into our driveway, exhausted, just after midnight, we discovered a strange car parked in our garage and the lights on in our dining room.

"Oh my God," Julia said. "Someone's broken in."

We were returning home from five miserable days in Jamaica, where the sand was so hot I sprouted blisters on my feet the size of soup spoons. We thought the trip might save our marriage. Why we thought this remains a mystery. We hadn't spoken to one another now for three days, an accomplishment, really, since we'd shared a hotel room and had just flown side by side for three hours in a DC 10.

I recognized the car in our garage, a black Saab with the tail lights shattered, the rear seat, I knew, full of canvases, paint brushes, and hundreds of skinny brown sticks which had once been McDonald's french fries. Andrew.

Julia said, "We should call the police."

I got out of the car and walked to the front door. Julia followed me. Shards of broken glass sparkled on the concrete stoop.

I grabbed the doorknob and turned it. Julia touched my arm.

"Are you crazy!" she asked.

I looked at her.

"You're right," I said. "You first." A bad, mean-spirited joke.

"Fuck you, Frank," she said.

I went in, Julia trailing behind.

In the dining room, our plush, ivory-colored carpeting was splat-tered with oil paint of every conceivable color. Globs of darker and lighter colors congealed like seagull droppings. The dining room chairs, thankfully, were arranged in a little train down the hallway. But our cherry table rested on thick pillars of books stacked some three feet high, so that the top of the table itself reached near the ceiling. A wooden stepladder, also dotted with paint, stood next to the table. My colleague and friend Andrew, an art professor at the university, lay on his back above us, whistling the opening notes from Wagner's *Ride of the Valkyries* over and over, his bare feet poking over the edge of the table, dotted with yellows and blues and darker pigments.

Our dining room ceiling, antique white when we left for Jamaica, now depicted a reproduction of Michelangelo's Sistine Chapel fresco, the *Creation of Adam*. A well-nourished and muscular God, reclined in nude splendor, his long black hair braided into Rastafarian dreadlocks, was reaching out to pass a thick marijuana joint to the figure of Adam, who reached for it with a smile on his face. Andrew's God was black, and he had a penis over eighteen inches long.

"Andrew," I said, "Did you have to break our window?"

"There was no key under the doormat, Frank. What kind of Americans are you?"

"Jesus Christ," Julia said. "I don't believe this."

Andrew slowly rolled to the side and peered down at us.

"Hey," I said. "What's going on?"

He rolled to his stomach, squirmed down the table toward the lad-der. The towers of books wobbled unsteadily. Only when Andrew's feet found the ladder and he descended did we learn that he wasn't wearing any clothes. His body was splattered in oils, too, colored skid marks down his back and bottom, and candied dots clinging to his face, to the hair on his legs and chest, and matted like syrup in his pubic hair. From its rack on the wall, I grabbed one of the flowery plates Julia's grandmother had given her and handed it to Andrew. He looked at the plate and then at me. I nodded at his privates. He covered himself.

I stared at the ceiling. "God's dick is bigger than a Budweiser bottle, Andrew," I said.

He smiled. "Well, he's GOD, you know? The Father. He should look virile."

"Uh-huh," I said. I looked at Julia. She looked ready to blow. If there were a seismograph wired to her brain, the needle would have been twitching up into the eights or nines. Julia is Vesuvius in pastel, cotton-polyester blends.

"I used a slide to project the outline." Andrew touched the paintbrush to one of his fingernails. "I just finished varnishing. It'll keep the colors from fading." He pointed to the picture window. "You should put in a smaller window here. Sunlight's going to be a killer on this."

Julia glared at me and then at Andrew. "What?" Andrew said to her. "This place is a monochromatic hell! All these white walls and ceilings, I felt like a chick inside an eggshell. Frank, you said if things ever got really bad I could crash here, so I'm crashed." He shifted his weight from one foot to the other, like someone standing on really hot sand.

"How long since you've slept?" I asked him.

"Tuesday," he said. "Maybe. What day is it now?"

"Sunday," I said. Julia counted on her fingers.

"Six days?" Julia said. "You haven't slept in six days?"

"Is that what it's been?" Andrew asked. He shrugged his shoulders. "I'm all out of blow, too."

"Cocaine?" Julia said, shrilly. "Cocaine? You've been doing drugs in our house?"

"What what?" Andrew asked. "You always say everything twice twice?"

"I want him out," Julia said. She turned on her heel to walk toward our bedroom. "Tonight, Frank. Out." The door slammed.

"Out out," Andrew said. "Isn't that something from literature?"

"Thanks for pissing off my wife, Andrew. Like we don't have enough problems."

"Well, *is* it literature, Frank?" Andrew asked.

"Yes. 'Out, out, brief candle! Life's but a walking shadow, a poor player that struts and frets his hour upon the stage, and then is heard no more.' *Macbeth*."

"Such erudition!"

"It's the title of a Frost poem, too. About the kid with the chainsaw."

"You amaze me."

"Fuck off, Andrew. Get some clothes on and tell me what happened."

Andrew's my best friend, whatever that means for two men in their late thirties with university teaching jobs and tenure. Not much, maybe. We play racquetball together. Sometimes we teach together, a course called Literature and the Visual Arts. Paintings and poems about paintings, as Andrew calls it. The three little pees. His clothes were piled on the floor beneath the table, and he dropped to his knees to reach for them. I walked into the kitchen. "You want something to eat?" I shouted to him. I opened the refrigerator door. In addition to the food we'd left when we went on vacation were five large jars of peanut butter and several loaves of Wonder bread. The first time Andrew and his wife separated he ate nothing but french fries for three months.

He padded into the kitchen barefoot, wearing faded blue jeans and a white t-shirt. "I had a peanut butter sandwich about an hour ago," he said.

"You smell a little ripe," I said.

"You Americans," he answered, "always hung up on cleanliness."

"You're an American, Andrew," I said.

"That's true," he answered, "but I'm a bad American, not the Ugly American. I don't count. How was your vacation?"

"Awful."

"Write up a treatment for Hollywood," he said. "Maybe it would make a good movie."

"I think I'm having a midlife crisis."

"Nonsense," Andrew said. "You're not old enough."

I nodded and took a deep breath. "And what about you? How have you been?"

Andrew shook his head. "Not well," he said. "Not well at all."

We talked until four in the morning. Andrew's sister had been dying of breast cancer in Atlanta. Weeks earlier, he had planned to fly down from Chicago to visit her, but at the airport he suddenly decided the planes looked unairworthy—"so heavy," he said, "all that silver metal sparkling in the sun, thousands and thousands of pounds. It just dawned on me that human flight must be a scam, Wilbur and Orville Wright just some conspiracy fairy tale to indoctrinate children into buying Supersaver fares as adults. And I thought, what if I'm up there and everyone stops believing all at once? I mean, down we come, like that jet over Lockerbie, our body parts, our clothes and condoms scattered all over people's back yards."

The blaze of Andrew's year-long affair with a young woman named Nicola had again consumed him. She had been his student, a beautiful, talented young painter, but self-destructive, and, at twenty-two, almost half his age. Worse: Nicola was the daughter of another faculty member on campus, Professor White in the College of Business, a formidable woman who wore power suits and shoes with stiletto heels rumored to be so sharp they could penetrate a man's thoracic cavity.

"You're crazy," Andrew's friends told him at the time.

"Tell me something everyone doesn't know," he answered.

"But Carol White's *daughter!*" we said. "You'll lose your job, your wife, your house, your reputation. You'll lose everything."

"'Everything' is not a list of four things," Andrew said.

"What do you see in her, to risk that list of four things?" I asked him.

"If you have to ask," he said, "then you've never seen it for yourself."

Andrew's wife Linda eventually discovered that he was seeing Nicki. She found motel charges on their Visa statement. She confronted Andrew. He denied it, said someone must have stolen his credit card. She opened his wallet and found his credit card. He said the thief must have put it back. Thieves are clever people, he said. The good ones are like sprites, spirits, fairies.

"This love with Nicki," he said. "It's a force of nature, a Level Five hurricane, a flood. And the sex, Frank. She does anything, everything. And we talk all night afterward, about real things, about real life, the stuff inside that you keep hidden away so you can do ordinary stuff— go to work, buy Italian loafers, order fries at McDonald's—without shooting yourself in the head."

But because Andrew was married, this love for Nicki was nitro-glycerin in a cracked jar. Once Andrew tried to break it off with her, but she kicked in the brake lights of his car. "The brake lights deal was like a metaphor," he said. "She didn't want to stop." He went back to her. Then she broke it off. Went back. "As the moon pulls the tides," he said. "It's unavoidable." The Saturday Julia and I left for Jamaica, Andrew moved out of his wife's house and into Nicki's one-bedroom apartment.

Andrew looked down at the kitchen table, picked some paint from the back of his hand. "Last week Annie died," he said. "My mother called from Atlanta on Saturday morning. She *screamed* at me." He held an imaginary phone to his ear. "'Why didn't you come down here? You're the only one she ever wanted to see! She died with your name on her lips!' Breast cancer at thirty-eight." He wiped tears from his face with the palms of his hands. "So I just thought, fuck it."

"I'm sorry."

He shook his head. "Annie was my *twin*," he said.

"I know."

"So I went to Nicki's. But Linda followed me there," he said. "How the hell was I supposed to know she'd track me down like some lioness following a blood trail? Somehow she got into the building and started knocking on the door. 'I know you're in there!' she kept screeching. 'Open up this goddamn door, Andy! I know you're in there!' Scared the shit out of me. Nicki and I were huddled down in the bedroom trying to think of what to do. And then the banging stopped, and pretty soon we could see Linda outside on the patio. She had her hands cupped over her face and was peering through the glass door. And she starts shouting again, 'Open up this goddamn door! I'm not leaving!' With her hands over her face that way, she looked like a giant fruit bat or something! Well then she turns around and picks up one of these cast-iron lawn chairs—the black ones, you know, really, really heavy—and she lets out this scream like an East German shot-putter on performance-enhancing drugs and tosses that chair—I mean throws it like she means *business*, all pumped with adrenaline she could have lifted a railroad car off the tracks—and that chair comes crashing through the patio-door glass, bounces off the end table, and lands upright next to the sofa, not a piece of glass on it. Someone could have sat right down on it. I was in awe."

"No shit? Then what?"

"Well, Nicki locked herself in the bedroom and called the police. Who could blame her? When Linda came through that broken door she didn't look like a fruit bat anymore, she looked like Linda Blair in *The Exorcist* with her head spinning around. Scary, man. And before the police got there, I went back home with Linda. I mean, what was I supposed to do? A woman breaks through patio-door glass to get to you, I don't think you have any choice in the matter. You have to go with her. It's like the law of the jungle, or something. But when Linda finally fell asleep, sometime the next morning, I came over here. I've been here ever since. I didn't know where else to go."

"Does Linda know you're here?"

He shook his head. "She thinks I'm in Panama."

"Panama?"

He shrugged. "Yeah, I called her and she asked me where I was and I just said Panama. I don't know why I said that. We don't even own the Panama Canal anymore, did you know that? Jimmy Carter gave it away. Lucky he wasn't a Republican, or he would have given them the Grand Canyon. Piss off the environmentalists. Give Al Gore a stroke—though who would notice?"

"So you came over to my house and destroyed my dining room."

"Oh come on, Frankie. You love that painting. Tell me you love it."

"I love it. But our carpeting doesn't look so hot."

"No, you're right," Andrew said, "you'll have to get new carpeting." He paused. "And you'll have to get somebody to refinish the top of that table. Is that mahogany?"

"Cherry. Very expensive."

He nodded. And then he got up and walked into the living room, where he laid down on the floor, went to sleep, and didn't get up, except to go to the bathroom, until Tuesday morning. He could have slept all week, since he didn't need to be anywhere. He was on a semester's LOAH from the university—Leave of Absence for Health reasons. Instead of "loah," Andrew called it a luau, "but without the roast pig and grass skirts," he said.

"He's off his meds, and he's having some problems," I said, softly, to Julia, Monday morning, as we ate breakfast and sucked down black coffee that burned our tongues. We both pretended not to smell the paint fumes emanating from the dining room. I had slept just two hours. My eyes felt like open wounds packed with sand. "He's my friend, Julia."

"*We're* having problems, Frank," Julia said. "Has that little detail escaped you? What's more important to you, your marriage or your friendship with that statutory rapist-pornographer?"

"Nicki's twenty-two," I said. "That hardly makes him a rapist."

Julia rolled her eyes at me. "Oh, twenty-two!" she said. "Goodness! Put her on estrogen."

"You're clever when you're hostile."

"Fuck you."

"Don't do this," I said. "Please. Don't make me choose. Not right now."

"Oh for God's sake, Frank," Julia said. "Jamaica was supposed to be romantic! But it was like being at a shopping mall with my mother. Something's missing, Frank. Our marriage is AWOL. It is dying a slow death. It is moldy cheese on a stale cracker."

"You're mixing your metaphors."

"You are such an asshole."

"Look," I said, "Andrew's having a hard time. I'm not throwing him out."

"I'm calling Linda," she said. "I'm going to tell her he's here and she can come and get his paint-speckled ass out of my house."

"Don't," I said. "Please, don't. His twin sister died Saturday. The one in Atlanta. He just needs some time."

Julia sighed. She raised her hands briefly, as if in surrender. "A couple days," she said. "But then we have to talk."

"A couple days," I repeated.

"And then talk," Julia said. "Real talk."

"Talk, talk," I said. "Okay, okay."

Julia shook her head. "Don't push it."

Wednesday afternoon, my graduate seminar on Melville's *Moby-Dick* went badly. During our discussion, my mind wandered to my unhappy marriage, to Andrew, to the difficulties of sustaining love. One clever graduate student, a young man named Kris, who spelled his first name with a backwards "K," claimed Moby Dick might be a symbol of the white man's insecurity about the size of his penis. "Little dick, big whale," he said. "It makes sense."

"And what do the rest of you think of that theory?" I asked, my usual gambit when such preposterous ideas emerged.

"Do we know how big Melville's was?" someone else asked, snickering. The other students all looked at me blankly.

Are you *all* idiots? I thought to myself. "No, we don't," I said. I felt deflated. My teaching was going nowhere. "And that's the wrong question to ask."

"I don't think so," Kris said, shaking his mop of hair vigorously.

"Look," I said, "In the nineteenth century, people didn't use the word 'dick' to refer to a man's penis. That's a twentieth-century idiom."

"But he spends a whole page writing about a whale's dick in the book!" Kris said, furiously turning pages to find the passage. "It's like as big as a toddler, or something."

A thin, young woman with a pierced eyebrow slammed her book closed and stood up. "This is sexual harassment," she said.

"I'm reporting it."

Kris raised his arms. "What the fuck?" he said.

The young woman marched out of the room and slammed the door behind her.

I stared at the floor. I couldn't concentrate. Everyone stared at me. I could hear the wall clock ticking. Tears flooded my eyes.

"Professor?" someone asked. "You all right?"

"No," I said. "I'm not."

I found Andrew up on metal scaffolding in my living room, where we have a cathedral ceiling, two forty-five-degree angles that meet at an oak beam in the center, sixteen feet from the floor. He's got two-by-tens spread in a kind of catwalk across the scaffolding. Thankfully, plastic sheeting is taped to the floor and covering all of the furniture.

"Where's Julia?" I asked. "I need to talk to her."

"Ah," he said. "Julia. She left. She said maybe she'd go to a motel."

"She left me?"

"No," Andrew said, "she left *me*. She came home from work and saw me here and out she went. Well, we talked a little. I apologized for my 'out, out' crack on Sunday night. But if there had been glass in that front door she would have broken it."

"Christ, Andrew," I said. "You could have asked permission. This isn't your fucking playland."

"I'm sorry," he said. "You're pissed."

I sighed. "I had a bad day."

"I've got some Zoloft in my car," he offered. "Take it with gin. Calms you right down."

I shook my head and looked up at the ceiling.

"I'm thinking I'll paint a memorial to Annie," he said. "A real fresco, you know? Wet plaster and watercolors."

"Of what?"

"I don't know yet."

"Well, keep the penises to scale."

"You have no sense of visual adventure, Frankie." He laughed.

Andrew moved in and Julia moved out. Though I felt thankful to get a rest from the constant tension with Julia, I must admit, that first night, with Andrew humming to himself in the living room, leafing through art history books to find the appropriate painting to reproduce on the ceiling, I felt estranged, sad, even a bit panicked. Being in a longish marriage—for me going on 17 years—is like being in a house with the television on in another room. Even if you're not watching, the background noise is somehow comforting. Not the most romantic view of things, I realize.

That evening the telephone rang in the kitchen and I answered. Julia.

"Where are you?" I asked.

"I'm at Linda's," Julia said.

"Linda's?"

"I'm not here!" Andrew shouted from the living room.

"You didn't tell her," I said.

"No, no," Julia said. "Linda's not even home. She went out shopping. She says Andrew told her he's in Panama, for God's sake."

"I know. I heard."

"So where are *we*? It's him or me, Frank. I like Andrew, but I can't live in that house with him painting our ceilings and whistling Mahler."

"It's Wagner," I said.

"Oh, goddamn it, Frank!"

"Jules, it'll just be a week or so. Come back."

"No," she said. "I can't. It's late for us, Frank." Her voice quivered.

"Where are you going to go?"

"My mother's," she said. She paused. I didn't respond. "Well, okay then," she said. And she hung up.

"Julia," I said. I hung up the phone.

I walked into the living room. Andrew reclined on his back on a board near the top of the scaffolding, ten feet off the floor. An open art history book was on his chest. "I'm breaking up your marriage," he said.

"You might be the final straw," I said.

"Should I leave?" he asked.

"Where would you go?"

"I don't know."

"Stay then," I said. "Until you do."

"Thank you," he said. "If God runs heaven and Satan runs hell, who's at the gates of purgatory?"

"I don't know," I said. "Some middleman, I guess."

"No, it's you, Frank. You're the man in the middle. You're the middleman."

Two days later when I came home from work I found Andrew sitting on the kitchen floor in the middle of six twelve-packs of Mountain Dew. He looked as if he had been crying.

"I talked to Nicki today," he said. "Her voice makes this big mud slide go off inside my chest. I want to be with her so badly." He ran his hands through his hair and shook his head. His fingers quivered. "Why does a love this big come when things are all wrong for it?"

"So, go to her."

"Not that easy," he said. "You know what my shrink told me? He said having a love affair is like juggling chain saws. It's a rush and it makes your heart pound, but sooner or later you find your hands on the floor and you're spurting blood from both wrists."

"That's a pleasant image."

"Don't you ever wish you could be in two places at once? Wouldn't it be wonderful? When Annie was alive, because we were twins, I sometimes felt a little like I was in two places at once, you know? I could be here in Chicago *and* in Atlanta. And now that she's dead, I don't know." He crossed his arms. "I feel more finite."

"If we *could* be in two places at once, Andrew, we'd want to be in four places," I said. "It's human nature. But in relationships you have to choose just one place. It's the law of marriage."

"Not for Mormons."

"So convert."

He rolled his eyes. "The desert air in Provo is way too dry," he said. He crossed his legs. "What's it like being married to Julia?"

"Right now, it feels like we're beating a dead horse, trying to make it get up and run."

"That sounds awful."

"It's not that unusual," I said. "If you look up and down this street, there's a horse's skeleton in every manicured back yard. The Chem-Lawn man has to walk around it every time he comes to fertilize the fescue and kill the weeds."

"No," Andrew said. "Some of those people are in love, Frankie."

"Maybe," I said. "But maybe love is just a few brain chemicals out of whack. Maybe it's just self-deception."

"No!" Andrew shouted. "No, Frank! That's not right! Love can be like riding bareback along the rim of a canyon. At a gallop. On a blind, epileptic horse. At night. Forever."

"The sun will come up," I said. "The horse will get tired. It'll slow to a walk. It will die. The vultures will start to circle."

"When did you get so cynical?" Andrew asked.

"Realism isn't cynicism, Andrew. It might be the gravy you serve with cynicism, but it's not the same thing."

"I disagree."

"You disagree. Remember Charlie Lester, the guy in Psychology?"

"The vegetarian?"

"Yeah. Remember his dog, that yellow lab he named Corn Cob? He said he was going to raise that dog a vegetarian, have him eat lower on the food chain. Corn Cob was going to be the first vegetarian carnivore on the face of the earth. And remember what happened to that dog? Charlie fed him asparagus and green beans and potatoes and carrots all covered with gravy so the dog would actually eat the stuff. And it got sick and died. The PETA people at the university found out about it and there was an investigation. Charlie almost got indicted, for God's sake."

"So what's your point?"

"My point is, Andrew, there's the real world. There's the law of gravity. There's $E = mc^2$. Dogs eat meat. There are certain things we cannot change."

He shook his head and sighed. "That's a creed I cannot live by, Frank."

"It's reality," I said.

"Not mine," he said.

"When apples fall from the tree, they hit the ground. They don't float away."

"They're all just following the herd," Andrew said. "But not me. Not me, Frankie."

The fresco Andrew decided upon for our living room ceiling was Michelangelo's *Temptation and Expulsion of Adam and Eve*. It fit our ceiling perfectly, he said. The oak beam in the middle would become the tree of knowledge, with the serpent's tail wrapped around it like a Slinky.

I handed the book back to him. "This is beautiful," I said.

"I'll start in the morning," he said. "My guess is it'll take a week or two. Maybe less. Depends how much I sleep. I'm going to put my sister's face on Eve. I hope you don't mind."

"Not at all."

"My mother's face is going on the serpent."

I nodded. "Nice touch."

"How's Julia?"

"I don't know," I said. "I haven't talked to her. Her mother's answering machine is on and no one's picking up."

"I called Linda today. I put crinkled wax paper over the telephone and put a Spanish opera on your stereo. She was impressed how clear my voice could be from so far away. I felt a little guilty." He pinched the index finger and thumb of one hand together. "Just a little. I told her how impressed I was that she could throw a lawn chair through that patio door. If the Olympics had that event, she'd win the gold medal, I told her. The manager of the apartment complex is suing her for damages. Nicki took out a restraining order. She's afraid of Linda."

"That's understandable," I said.

"I don't know what it is about Linda," Andrew said. "I mean, given our present married life, leaving it wouldn't be that hard for me. But hurting another person, that's hard, Frankie. And in marriage, it's not always the present but the past and the future that hold you, right? The years of history you have, and the fictional future years that just sort of construct themselves in your mind when you're not paying attention—retiring, getting your AARP cards, getting ten percent off your meals together at Burger King. Shit like that."

"Uh-huh," I said.

"Don't you think about that with Julia?" he asked.

"No," I said, "I don't. I don't think about anything as much as you do, Andrew."

"You should, Frank," he said. "You really should. An unexamined life is not worth living."

"Schopenhauer says no life is worth living."

"Yes, well, he lived in the days before Prozac," Andrew said. "If Schopenhauer were alive today, he'd change his tune."

Days passed. The wash didn't get done. The shopping didn't get done. The dishes piled up. This was not a problem for Andrew, who had one set of clothes he never took off and plenty of peanut butter, white bread, and Mountain Dew. Andrew said when the washing machine spun out in the laundry room, which was off the kitchen, the living room ceiling quivered. So I had to work around his painting and plastering schedule. And I couldn't use the sink when it was full of plaster, which was most of the time.

The University's Sexual Harassment Task Force made an appointment to meet with me to discuss complaints about my Melville Seminar. They sent Carol White to my office to gather my view of the facts. I tried not to stare at her shoes. She said a student complained that my teaching was penis-centered. Carol said this with a straight face. I replied this was false, that we tried to focus on a different body part each week.

"I know my daughter is seeing Andrew Blakely," Carol said.

I shrugged. "Love blinds us."

She shook her head. "Sex is what blinds us," she said. "My daughter is sick. He's twice her age."

"Andrew's sick, too."

"Then they're a perfect match, aren't they?" Carol said.

"I'm sorry," I said. "I don't know what to tell you."

"What happened in your Melville seminar?"

"Someone asked if I knew the size of Melville's penis. We were discussing *Moby-Dick* at the time."

She shook her head, depressed by the depths to which literary scholarship had fallen. Postmodernists had ruined everything. "That's it?"

I nodded.

"Tell Blakely to leave my daughter alone." She closed her notebook and left my office.

The next evening I ran into Linda in the grocery store. I was in the produce aisle looking at all the exotic fruits and vegetables. Linda looked good. She wore a yellow dress, and her brown hair was up off of her neck.

"Frank!" Linda said, ramming my shopping cart with hers, with what seemed like undue force. I respected her strength now, certainly.

Because it seems an invasion of privacy to stare at someone else's groceries, I averted my eyes from her cart. In my own cart I had a stack of frozen TV dinners ten-deep, five Salisbury steaks and five fried chickens, and four or five pieces of yet unnamed, exotic produce.

"Linda!" I said. "Hello." I tried to pretend Andrew wasn't at that moment on his back painting a Michelangelo on my living room ceiling. The more I tried not to think about it, the more I thought about it. Another law of the universe.

Linda said, "You look like you've had some sun."

"Julia and I just got back from Jamaica."

"Yes, she told me. How are things between you two?"

I considered lying, but I didn't know if I could keep two fairly substantial lies going in the air at the same time. Something like that takes talent. "We're separated," I said. "She's staying at her mother's for awhile."

Linda said, "I'm so sorry."

I shrugged. "I'm hanging in there. And how's Andrew?" I asked. I couldn't resist.

"Andrew's in Panama," she said.

"Panama!" That I said this with a straight face was no less than a miracle.

"Well, who knows? It's been a little rough for us, lately, too."

I nodded.

"Well," Linda said, backing her shopping cart away from mine, "I've got to get home. I hope things work out for you and Julia. For the both of us, I guess."

"I hope so, too," I said. Hope Springs Eternal, I thought. Hot Springs Inferno.

There was a red Dodge Neon in the driveway when I returned home. Andrew met me in the kitchen. I told him I'd seen Linda.

"How did she look?" Andrew asked, his voice soft and furtive.

"You look different," I said.

"I showered."

I slid nine of the frozen TV dinners into the freezer and one of them into the microwave. I poured the fruit and vegetables out on the table.

"She looked like she always looks," I said. "Did Julia call?"

"No," Andrew said. "Sorry."

I forced a smile and pointed to the produce I'd purchased. "What are these?"

He looked down at the five pieces of produce and touched them, one by one. "This is an avocado. These two are kiwi."

"They looked like big testicles, so I bought two."

Andrew smiled. "This one's a mango. And this is a pomegranate."

"How do you know all this?"

"I'm a painter, Frank."

"And how's the painting coming?" I asked. I moved to leave the kitchen to go into the living room.

Andrew raised his arm to block the door. He put his face close to my ear. "Nicki's here," he whispered.

"I saw the car in the driveway," I whispered back.

Andrew whispered, "My heart's pounding like a hummingbird's. Three hundred beats a minute, or whatever it is. God she is so amazing."

We went into the room and Andrew introduced us. I had seen Nicki before, of course, at the university when she was still a student. She was a beautiful young woman, small, muscular, with an exotic aura that made her seem a bit dangerous. Her hair was brown and curled, and her face was thin, angular, and without make-up. She looked a bit like her mother. She wore a white camisole and cut-off blue jeans, a gold stud in her pierced belly button. She had the words, "The Brain is Wider than the Sky," the first line of an Emily Dickinson poem, tattooed on one of her shoulders. She wasn't wearing any shoes. A series of short, parallel slices, scabbed over, extended down the tops of her arms. They looked like little, bloody ladders. She would have liked Sitting Bull, who offered up a sacrifice of fifty pieces of his flesh before the Battle of Little Bighorn, tiny slivers of meat carved from his arms. I curbed my impulse to tell her this.

It was easy to see what Nicki and Andrew saw in one another. They were open windows. Flocks of migrating birds could pass through their chests. Theodore Roethke had people like Nicki and Andrew in mind when he wrote, "Those who are willing to be vulnerable move among mysteries." It made me wonder if love requires an unstable medium to root properly, sort of the way certain orchids can only germinate in the canopy of tropical trees, the spores delivered there by hurricanes. It doesn't make things promising for those among us who are more earthbound.

Andrew, Nicki, and I chatted until the bell went off on the microwave, signaling that my Salisbury steak and mashed potatoes were hot.

"I'm going to eat, Andrew," I said, "and then I'm going to go out for the night."

"No, Frank. You don't have to do that. This is your house."

"I'm driving out to DeKalb to see Julia."

Andrew shrugged and nodded. "All right."

"The ceiling's looking great," I added. It was over half done. The "Temptation," side and the serpent looked nearly finished. The "Expulsion" side had been started. "Nicki," I said, "wonderful to see you again."

She nodded but didn't say anything. She looked sad.

I drove through the dark on 88 to DeKalb and found myself standing on the porch of Julia's mother's house thinking I should turn around and go back home. The television was on so loudly I could hear it clearly from the driveway.

I rang the doorbell. Julia answered. She looked lovely. She had her hair pinned up off of her neck and cotton balls stuffed in her ears.

"Frank," she said. She stepped back and invited me in.

"I want to talk," I said.

"If we stay here, we'll have to shout," she answered.

"Who is it?" her Mother screeched.

"Come in and say hi," said Julia. I nodded.

Julia turned down the television while I spoke loudly to her mother, then Julia put on her shoes and grabbed a coat, and we left the house to go for a walk. It was about forty degrees, a cool night for April in northern Illinois. The skies were clear and filled with stars.

Julia grabbed my hand, and I let her hold it. Once, long ago, when our flesh touched, it was as if a small electric charge had been generated. Layers of insulation had since grown between us.

"We can call this a walk talk," I said. "If it's a short one, we'll say it's a walkie talkie."

"No hiding behind words," said Julia. "That's all you ever do."

"Do I?" I asked.

She nodded.

"How about Wok Talk?" I added. I spelled out the letters. "Our motto could be stir fry or die. Or I'll try and you'll sigh. Or bye, bye Miss American pie."

Julia angrily dropped my hand.

"I'm afraid of intimacy," I said.

"You make jokes about everything," Julia said, tears coming to her eyes. "I can't even talk to you anymore."

"Books say it's a defense mechanism."

"Books can't be trusted."

"People can't be trusted," I said.

"But at least you can look them in the eye."

"Only when they're awake."

"Christ, Frank," she said. "How did we get to this point?"

"I don't know," I said. "But we're here." I went on talking, though. I told her everything that had happened in the eight days that she'd been gone. I told her about my Melville seminar, the sexual harassment complaint, Andrew's painting. Then the conversation turned. We talked about things we'd done together, places we'd traveled over the past seventeen years. We walked for nearly two hours, sat down on the curb in front of her Mother's house when we got tired of walking, our warm breath pouring in visible clouds from our mouths.

"What happened to us?" I asked her, finally. "It's like we're oxygen and hydrogen. Mix us together, and you get water."

"Water's the foundation of all life."

"But it's not very exciting," I said. "Sure, it goes from ice to steam, but that's not much range, given the extremes of the larger universe."

"What are you saying to me, Frank?"

"I don't know what I'm saying. I want to feel more than I feel. Andrew's in love. I want to feel that again. I just feel sad. All the time."

"Andrew's mentally ill," Julia said.

"The same thing, maybe. But I want it."

"Are you saying you no longer love me?"

"I don't know what I'm saying."

"It sounds like that's what you're saying." Julia seemed as if she might cry.

"It just seems like we've been skipping across the surface of things all these years."

"I don't know what that means, Frank."

I shrugged. "It's my fault," I said. "I'm sorry." I felt then that maybe our marriage really might be over, that we had crossed some invisible continental divide and we were tumbling down the other side of the mountain. My stomach churned. Julia began crying. I thought about our early years, happy afternoons of sex on a sunny, carpeted floor beneath the bedroom window, the promise of the future, the hope for children that we never got around to having, the weeks we spent vacationing in Europe, in China, in the Caribbean. What goes wrong?

I said, again, "I'm sorry."

Julia put her face into her hands and sobbed. I could have put my arm around her in comfort, could have sat with her for awhile longer. But I couldn't take it, couldn't take sitting there in the dark, feeling sick and tired and hopeless. I fled the scene. I got up, went to my car, started it, and drove away with a fierce aching in my chest.

All the way back to Elmhurst, I kept checking in my rear view mirror to see if Julia's car was behind me. I didn't know what I would do if she followed me back home, but I didn't have to worry about that, because she didn't.

I got home after one a.m. The red Neon was gone. The lights in the living room were on, and through the front windows, I could see the partially finished painting on the ceiling.

I went into the house. Andrew was sitting cross-legged on the living room floor, his hands together, his body rocking forward and back, hypnotically.

"Andrew?" I said. He looked up at me. Purple smudges ringed his eyes. He ran his right thumb hard in a circle against his left palm, over and over and over, pushing so hard his thumbnail flashed red. He had worn through the skin already. Beneath the thumb, his hand was smeared with blood.

"Nicki left you," I said.

Andrew nodded. "She wanted to be a work of art," he said. "She wanted to be adored." He shook his head. "I told her, 'Honey, I'm sorry, but even the Venus de Milo has a few chips in her marble ass.'"

I laughed and he smiled, weakly.

"It was the wrong thing to say," Andrew said.

I shrugged. "Maybe she had it coming."

Andrew looked down at his hand, at his thumb circling in his own blood. "I called Linda," he said. "I'm going to go to the hospital for a little while."

"I understand," I said. I looked up at the unfinished painting. Even in the dim light, it looked bright and beautiful. Eve looked radiant and alive. "Maybe it's all Eve's fault," I said.

Andrew looked up at me, then at the ceiling. He shook his head. "No," he said. "No, that's not right. Adam jumped right in, too. He wasn't going to let Eve have all of the fun. A good thing doesn't stay good for long, Frankie. It just gets more interesting."

Headlights flashed across the living room window and lit up the front yard. A car stopped in the driveway. A door slammed. "Linda's here," I said.

I met her at the door. Linda looked tired. I quickly apologized for allowing her to believe Andrew had been in Panama.

"Oh for Christ's sake, Frank," Linda said. "How stupid do you think I am? I saw his car in your garage days ago. I figured at least if he was here, he was safe."

"But I *was* in Panama!" Andrew said to Linda. He held up his bloody hand. "Panamanian rebels did this. They wanted my Nikes."

"Where's Julia?" Linda asked.

"At her mother's," I said. "I don't think she'll be back."

"No?"

I shrugged. "I'm not sure," I said.

Linda kissed me on the shoulder and then helped Andrew get to his feet. "Come on Michelangelo," she said. "They've got a bed waiting for you." She hooked a hand around one of Andrew's arms and led him slowly to the front door. Andrew walked like a small child pulled from bed in the middle of the night. Linda helped him put on his coat.

"Linda," I said.

"What?" She turned to face me.

"Why do you stay with him?"

She looked at Andrew. She took in a slow, deep breath, then exhaled. She smiled. "He's a bad habit, I guess."

"You should take up smoking," Andrew said. "It's healthier."

I said, "Let me drive you both to the hospital."

"That's not necessary," Linda said.

"I want to," I said. "Please."

"Follow us, if you want," Linda said. I did.

By the time I returned home, it was nearly three in the morning. My stomach knotted when I saw Julia's car parked in our driveway. I parked my car in the garage next to Andrew's and went into the house. But I couldn't find Julia. I looked in every room, even called to her in the basement.

In the living room, I stared up at Andrew's unfinished painting.

Michelangelo's Garden of Eden. Temptation on the left. The expulsion on the right. And in the center the serpent, calling, calling, and calling. A good thing doesn't stay good for long.

I put on my coat and went outside. I found Julia in her car, curled in the back seat, asleep, covered by her winter coat. For a long while I stood on the driveway in the cold night air and stared at her through the window. In sleep, she looked beautiful in the familiar way a wife of many years can be beautiful, though she stirred in me no ardent physical desire. I looked across my yard at the other houses in the neighborhood, at the steady stream of porch lights that ran down the street like a necklace of good luck charms. What's the secret? I wondered. I had no idea.

Slowly, I opened the car's back door. I gently lifted Julia's legs and sat down. I lowered her legs against my thighs. She moaned softly. Quietly, I pulled the car door closed and then gently placed my arm across Julia's knees. I closed my eyes. Dawn would soon come, with its multicolors and complications, its necessary conversations. But for now I felt only the allure of the darkness, heard only the sounds of me and Julia breathing together, the smoky vapor of our breath coating the windows until we could no longer be seen from the outside.

Love in an Expanding Universe

Driving home afterward was always the most difficult part. The storm of lust which had blown through David's body had faded, as it always did, and he now felt fragmented, adrift, unadorned. He bore through the world distracted and disconnected, lulled by the drone of radial tires on concrete, the rhythmic, metronomic ticking of each seam in the highway, the stitching of white stripes along the centerline. Above him, the Milky Way stretched out like a black umbrella full of holes. Behind him, Amy followed in her white Audi, their little adulterous train, until she flashed her headlights twice—goodbye, I love you—and exited toward her sleeping husband and children.

David watched her fade in his rear view mirror. Alone, now, he drifted toward his own wife and children, lost in the darkness between his two lives. Maybe he'd turn the radio on, sing along awkwardly to songs he half knew. Maybe he'd open the *Camry* windows, let the night air pour through the car. Maybe he'd cry. It all depended. But all the way home, the evening's memories would taunt him like the phantom pain of an amputated limb: the scent of Amy's skin, the tug of her thick, dark nipples under his tongue, the force of her cries as she came. Desperation, she said, was the ultimate aphrodisiac.

"I would die for you," David had whispered, afterward, his arm encircling her bare shoulders.

Amy had laughed playfully, quoting Shakespeare, "Men have died from time to time and worms have eaten them, but not for love." To Amy, an English professor David had met at a Women's Shelter fund-raiser coordinated by his wife, Janine, Shakespeare remained life's only unimpeachable source of wisdom. Hurt, David frowned. Amy gently bit his lip, moved her mouth to his ear. "Oh love," she whispered, "listen to yourself. You won't even leave your wife."

"But I *would* die for you," David repeated. Pathetic, he knew.

Amy sighed, rolled to her back, the summer white of her breasts glowing brightly against her tanned ribcage and belly, a sprinkling of freckles across her clavicles and breastbone. Each time they lay together afterward, in the warm, sexual scent of their bodies, she told David they were setting the stage for tragedy. In the end, she said, someone must be betrayed. It was adultery's only law.

David's wife, Janine, dropped into his thoughts uninvited, a silent flush of fallen leaves. David loved Janine, yes, but without desperation, a tranquilizing kind of love that did not calamitously disrupt his sense of the world's order. He'd been aware of this for some time. Several years earlier, to celebrate their tenth wedding anniversary, David and Janine had flown to Paris. On their first morning, still jet-lagged, they had waited in line outside of Notre Dame Cathedral with a busload of smiling Japanese tourists, whose necks sagged with huge, black cameras, the lenses as long as telescopes. David and Janine had purchased their tickets and together climbed the winding, limestone steps to the top of the cathedral. Walking among the gargoyles above the city, David had been enthralled, overwhelmed.

When he ducked inside the garret of massive wooden beams that housed the gargantuan, cast-iron bell, he suddenly felt, by contrast, the crushing smallness, the finiteness, of his own life. With their tiny instamatic camera, Janine took his photograph standing beside the bell, then joined the line of tourists heading back to the street. Later, at a souvenir shop on rue St. Michel, she had purchased a small, cast-iron cathedral paperweight. But David had stayed with the bell a long time, unable to leave, entranced to the point of tears, reaching to touch the cool, dark iron each time the bored, young Frenchman keeping watch looked away.

For David, being with Amy felt like that morning. She expanded his perceptions, opened his body and brain to a grandeur he could not name. With her, he felt unbounded. "That's just hormones, love," Amy said, when he tried to explain this to her. "Dopamine, norepi-nephrine, oxytocin. They're like drugs." She smiled at him.

"But what about love?" David asked.

"Such a *romantic* you are," Amy said. She reached for his penis, now soft and wrinkled as the pelt of some small, pale rodent. She looked sad. "To love another person is to see the face of God."

"Is that Shakespeare?"

She shook her head. "*Les Mis*," she answered. "Victor Hugo. The sap."

"Do you believe in God?" David asked. He ran the back of his hand over the smooth skin beneath Amy's navel, letting his fingers brush gently through tight curls of pubic hair.

"I'm Catholic," Amy answered. "I believe in everything."

David smiled. "Eternal damnation?"

Amy nodded. "Especially that," she said. "The eternal flames. A smoker's paradise." Amy shook her head and smiled. "I'm the paragon of inconsistency: a Catholic feminist having an affair."

"You make jokes about everything."

"It's a defense mechanism," Amy said. "A trick to keep my serotonin levels below the suicidal range."

"I love you," David said. He kissed her breast softly and she put a hand to the back of his head, held his hair in her fingers.

Amy said, "Love is the easy part, isn't it?"

David drove home to Janine at this hour, well after midnight, once every two weeks, on golf night. He would go golfing with three of his friends from the university where he taught marketing, but then afterward he would meet Amy at the Motel 6 over in Jackson, a 45-minute drive from home, pay in cash, endure the smirks of the wise-guy night clerk who would ogle Amy as she waited in the lobby. The clichéd mechanics of their affair, the hurried, parking-lot meetings, the cash payments, the king-sized motel bed with a black velvet painting of a matador hanging above the headboard, made David feel tawdry and ashamed. But when he and Amy closed their eyes, when their bodies came together, they entered a new and dazzling world.

In defense of his marriage, David knew Janine would say theirs was the kind of love that all love leads to, eventually—that every romance begins on hallowed ground but inevitably flows down a common grade into a common sea. That all love, finally, spills into a calm, inconspicuous pool with a neutral ph and the salinity of the human body at rest.

Pulling into his garage, his car lights cutting across the children's bicycles, the lawn mower, his wife's black VW bug, a knot of guilt and fear hardened in David's stomach. He felt like an intruder. He turned off the ignition, punched the garage door remote, left his car. Overhead, the steel door creaked down its galvanized tracks and met the concrete floor with a shudder.

Though he had showered at the motel with Amy, David showered again at home, then carefully lifted the covers and slid into bed beside Janine. He lay still, breathing softly, Janine's body heating the bed beneath a cotton sheet and a green acrylic blanket. This was the second most difficult part: moving from one bed into another, from one life into another. He closed his eyes, breathed shallow breaths, listened to the night sounds of the house, the roar of the gas water heater in the basement, the thumping of children's arms or legs against the wall as they rolled over in their beds.

He had begun to drift off when he sat up, startled by the ringing telephone. His brain in a fog, he reached for the receiver.

"Hello?" he said softly. Janine stirred, rolled over.

"David?" A man's voice, furtive, conspiratorial.

David's heart pounded, the blood a rush inside his ears. He asked, "Who is this?"

"It's me, Frank. Frank Altenbach." The overweight realtor who lived in the Cape Cod behind them with his wife and children. *Thank God*, David thought.

"Frank?" David said. His mind cleared and he looked at the clock, the bloody numbers glowing as if alive, beside the telephone. "Frank, it's one in the morning."

"I'm sorry," Frank said. "I really need your help." The noise that came next sounded like weeping.

"Frank, what's wrong?" David asked. He heard coughing, heavy breathing, wheezing.

"Look out your window," Frank said. He cleared his throat. "I'm on my cell."

David got out of bed. He tugged down on the shade, let it rise slowly. Beyond his children's swing set, over the unkempt privet hedge that separated his yard from the Altenbach's, David could see Frank standing near the middle of his own yard, one hand to his ear. Frank raised an arm.

"I see you," David said. "What's going on?"

"I'm trying to dig a hole," Frank said. "They built this neighborhood on a fucking gravel pit. Did you know that? We've got six inches of dirt, and underneath that is all rock."

"You're digging a hole?" David asked. "At this hour? You planting a tree?"

"Not a hole," Frank said. "Christ, no. I'm not planting a tree." He paused. "I'm trying to dig a grave."

Then David noticed a large, dark mound in the grass behind Frank's legs, something thick and heavy. My God, David thought. He's killed someone.

"I don't want the kids to wake up to this," Frank said. "I'm in a fucking panic over here, David."

David asked, "Have you called the police?"

"The police!" Frank shouted. "Christ no, David. Are you crazy? I don't want the police over here." Frank paced unsteadily. He staggered, almost fell, one arm flailing to help him keep his balance.

"Frank, are you drunk?"

"Am I drunk?" Frank repeated. "I don't know. Probably."

"Frank," David said. "What the hell's going on?"

Frank fell to his knees on the grass. He tried to stand, but tipped to his side and sat down. "Sally's dead," Frank whimpered.

"Sally?"

"Sally," Frank said, sadly. "My fucking dog."

"Your chocolate lab?"

"Yes," Frank said. "My beautiful, fucking dog."

David sighed, relieved. "Hang on, Frank," he said. "Give me a minute." He quietly hung up the telephone and looked at Janine. She appeared to be sleeping.

The July night felt unseasonable cool for Wisconsin, and David's slippered feet grew wet with dew as he crossed his yard and pushed through the hedge with a garden shovel balanced over one shoulder. A huge man with thinning hair, a thick, dark mustache that seemed to grow out of his nose, and hands the size of dinner plates, Frank sat on the ground with his shirt open, his large, hairy belly smeared with mud. Sally lay on her side beside him, thick as a dead seal, her stiff legs at right angles to her body. Frank stood up, and David shook his hand.

"Thanks for coming," Frank said. "You want a beer?" He nodded toward four cans of Budweiser in the grass.

"What the hell," David said. Frank opened two cans, gave one to David.

"I'm sorry about this," Frank said. "I didn't know who else to call. I saw your light on."

"Golf night," David said. He knelt at the dog's side and placed a hand on the fur over her ribs. Something dark and wet—blood?— matted the waxy, brown fur along her head and neck. "She get hit by a car?"

Frank shook his head. "She was old, almost blind, always bumping into furniture. Kept shitting on the floor."

David decided not to ask anything more. Some things you were better off not knowing.

Frank poked his shovel into the shallow hole he'd started digging. The blade scraped against stones and rock. "I've been out here half an hour," he said. "We'll need fucking dynamite to get this dog buried before sunrise."

David pointed to Frank's yard. "You got a half-acre here," he said. "We could try someplace else."

"No," Frank said, shaking his head deliberately. "No. I can look out the window from my chair and see this spot. I want her right here."

"You liked this dog."

"I loved this dog," Frank said. "Too much I loved this fucking dog. I'm never getting another one, I can tell you that. Go through this again? No, thank you."

They began digging, one man on each side of the hole. Gravel had compacted beneath the topsoil. The blades of their shovels scraped against stones, sent soft, orange sparks flickering into the darkness. Frank lost his balance, staggered and cussed. "Fuck," he said, each time his shovel hit a rock. Gradually, David's muscles warmed with the work, and the beer began to relax him. The earth gave off a pleasant, musky odor. In the distance, David heard crickets singing in the grass. He looked over at his own house, at the porch light illuminating the back door.

Once, he had loved his house, had loved everything about it. Lately, though, he found it held almost no appeal for him. Eight years ago, building it, moving in, had been the highlight of his life. Now that seemed strange to him. He wondered if other people felt this, too, felt formerly reliable enthusiasms wane. It happens as time speeds up to such a degree that life seems almost unlivable. You fall into habits, schedules, cycles: bills due the tenth of the month, trash pickup every Tuesday, kids' orthodontist's appointments once a month, dentist's office every six months, birthday parties every year. You discover that now that you have them, maybe you no longer want the things you wanted in your twenties and thirties. But you can't give them back. And then you find yourself digging a dog's grave with a drunken realtor in the middle of the night. Who could make sense of it?

"Fuck!" Frank huffed, slamming his shovel down in the wet grass. "I need a break." His body glistened with sweat that smelled like nicotine. He sat down and took a long drag from his beer, then lit a cigarette.

David dropped his shovel and sat down across from Frank.

They sat on opposite sides of the hole with their feet inside, their knees spread.

"You're a good man, David," Frank said. "I know me and my wife aren't the best neighbors."

"You're good neighbors," David said.

"We fight a lot, I realize," Frank said. "In the summer, windows open. People hear things."

David shrugged. This much was true. Their fights were operatic. The Divorce of Figaro, David sometimes called them.

"It didn't used to be that way," Frank said. "We didn't used to have so many problems, kids mouthing off, bills to pay. Christ, you know, sometimes I feel like I can't even fucking breathe. You ever feel that way?"

David nodded. "Sometimes." He took a long drink of beer. He tipped his head back, kept his eyes open, looked at the sky.

Frank sighed and looked up. "Look at all those goddamned stars," he said. "That's beautiful. I know the Big Dipper, that's all." He twisted his neck and almost tipped over backward. "Ah hell." He sat forward again. "It's up there somewhere."

"Scientists say the universe is getting bigger," David said. "They look in their telescopes, they do calculations that prove the stars and planets are all moving away from us. I heard that on public radio."

Frank blew out two huge lungs full of smoke, flicked his cigarette butt into the hole. "The universe is pretty fucking big already," Frank said.

David chuckled. "That's true," he said. "The stars are so far away, the light we see was emitted thousands of years ago. When we look at the stars, we're looking into ancient history." Frank grunted but didn't say anything. While back here on earth, David thought, our lives are shrinking. As we grow older, more and more possibilities disappear.

The thought depressed him. NPR depressed him. Maybe he should stop listening.

Frank said, "I heard once that we're all made of stardust, something like that."

David nodded. "Yeah. That's right. All the elements necessary for life are present in exploding stars. You listen to public radio?"

"Hell no." Frank shook his head. "I heard it in a Joni Mitchell song."

David laughed. They sat quietly for a few more minutes in the suburban quiet, finishing their beer. Frank belched, offered David another Budweiser, but David declined. Frank opened another one and chugged about half of it. They picked up their shovels and went back to work.

The hole grew deeper. Another twenty minutes passed. Frank stood over knee-deep in the dog's grave and David knelt on the side, bent over, the muscles in his back burning. A pile of stones and dirt had risen beside the hole.

Frank dropped his shovel and sat back down, his chest heaving. "Good enough," he said. "I'm going to have a fucking heart attack."

"We're just about there," David said.

Frank nodded. "Yeah, we'll be okay. We don't have to dig to China. I really appreciate your help." Frank wiped his mouth with the back of his hand. "Listen," Frank said. "Before you go, I should tell you. This dog did not die of natural causes."

"No?" David said.

"No," Frank said. "My wife, she killed this dog."

"She put her down on her own?" David asked.

"No," Frank said. He shook his head, vigorously. "No. We were having a fight. When we fight sometimes she just—I don't know. She isn't herself. She opened the kitchen drawer where we keep a bunch of tools, a couple screwdrivers, pliers, a hammer, to fix things around the house.

She pulled out the hammer. I thought she was going to hit me.
She was so goddamn mad. She walked over to where Sally was sleeping on the floor in front of the refrigerator, and she raised that hammer over her head. . . ."

"My God," David said.

Frank's lower lip began quivering. "Annie loved this dog, too.
More than me, even. Sally was our dog. We got her as a puppy, before we even had kids. She used to sleep in bed with us." Frank shook his head, slowly. "Sometimes, you know, I think we've forgotten every good thing we ever had between us." Frank drank the rest of his beer, squeezed the empty can flat in his hand, then tossed it into the grass.
He took a deep breath, blew it out, then put his face into his dirty, meaty hands and began to cry.

Embarrassed, David reached out to place one hand on Frank's shoulder but pulled it back.

Frank sniffled and sat up straight. "Fuck," he said. He wiped his face with the dirty tails of his open shirt. "It's the beer talking.
I'm sorry. I should stop fucking drinking."

"It's all right," David said.

Frank shook his head, raised one of his hands. "I'm fine," he said.
Frank leaned forward and tried to stand.

"I'm having an affair," David said, suddenly. It surprised him, how much he had wanted to say that, how forcefully the admission burst from his mouth.

"What?" Frank asked. He flopped back down.

"That's why I got home so late tonight," David said. "I was with another woman in a motel room over in Jackson."

Frank blinked. He seemed stunned. "No shit?" he said. He ran a hand through his thinning hair. "Wow." He looked at David's house.
"Does Janine know?"

David shook his head. "I don't think so."

"Wow," Frank said again. "I'm sorry. It's just kind of a shock, or something."

"I know," David said.

"What's it like?" Frank asked.

David said, "Some of it is incredible, the sex, lying around talking with her afterward. Touching her, smelling her. She's all I can think about. But the rest of the time," his thoughts trailed off. "I feel lost, I guess you might say."

"How long has this been going on?" Frank asked.

David thought back to when things started. "Eight or nine months."

"Is she married?"

David nodded. "She's—" he paused, seeking the proper words. "She's amazing. Her body, her brain, the things she says. I can't explain it."

"She hot?"

"She's beautiful," David said.

Frank nodded. "You said she says things," Frank said. "What kind of things?"

"Well," David said. "She quotes Shakespeare a lot. That's sort of intriguing. And the other night she said, 'A woman's clitoris is an iceberg.'"

Frank squinted his eyes. "Shakespeare said that?"

"No!" David laughed.

Frank chuckled. "I was thinking that wasn't the Shakespeare I read in school." He shook his head. "The clitoris is an iceberg," he repeated. He squinted at David. "What the hell does that mean?"

"I'm not sure," David said. "Maybe that what you see is just a small part of the whole. Maybe that a woman's body is complicated. It has connections to things we don't know, things that are deep and hidden."

David looked at Frank, whose face had slackened into a dull stare of incomprehension.

"Sounds kind of luny to me," Frank said. He suddenly grinned. "Hey," he said, pleased with himself, "you should have said your dick was the Titanic!"

David laughed.

Frank clapped his dirty hands. "Boom!" he said. "And then down you go, right to the bottom of the sea!"

"It feels that way sometimes," David said.

They laughed and moved their feet awkwardly over the gravel in the bottom of the hole.

"So what are you going to do?" Frank asked.

"I don't know."

"You going to leave Janine and your kids for this woman?"

David shook his head. The thought of that make him feel sick. But the thought of life without Amy made him feel hopeless. "I've gotten to a place where no matter what I do, I'm going to hate it."

They sat quietly for a while. Suddenly, Frank leaned toward David. David felt the weight of Frank's thick arm over his shoulders, across the back of his neck. Then Frank hugged him, hugged him so hard that David made a small, involuntary sound as the air was pushed from his lungs. Frank slapped him hard on the back. "You'll figure it out," Frank said. "Hate is a strong word. It can't be as bad as that."

"Thanks," David said. Frank lifted his arm over David's head and let it fall to his own lap. They looked at each other awkwardly.

"This has been a decent night, considering," Frank said.

David smiled. "Considering," he said.

"Well," Frank said, "I suppose we should bury this dog."

"You sure the hole is deep enough?" David asked.

"Yeah," Frank said. "What the hell. We'll pack her down good.

I'll go get Annie. She'll want to say goodbye."

Now that he had confessed to someone, David felt exposed, fearful, even regretful. He felt relieved he had told somebody but also wished he hadn't said anything. He didn't even know Frank all that well.

Frank slowly walked to his house and went inside to find his wife. David turned his attention to the dead dog in the grass. He dropped to his knees and bent at the waist, reached his arms around the body, placed his hands against the fur, now damp with dew. The dog had been overweight, eighty pounds, at least. David tried to lift the body, but it slid away from him, slippery as a chunk of wet ice. The palms of his hands darkened with thick, coagulated blood. He wiped them on the grass.

David glanced over at Frank's house. He grabbed Sally by the legs, one in each hand, and slid backward on his knees, dragging her body toward the hole. He pulled until her legs hung in the air over the grave. Then he crawled around behind and pushed her in. She rolled once and settled stiffly on her side, hidden now, in the darkness, underground.

He became aware of a sudden brightness behind him. He turned his head and saw a square of golden light shining from his bedroom window. Janine stood in the glass, lit from behind. Her features hidden in shadows, David could see only her dark silhouette. She seemed to be watching him, but he couldn't be certain. He pretended not to see, pretended to look elsewhere.

He heard Frank's patio door slide open, and he watched as Frank and his wife, Annie, emerged from their house. They walked gingerly through the wet grass, holding hands, their heads down, as if they had to avoid stepping on something dangerous.

"Okay," Frank said, when they reached David. "We're ready."

David nodded. Annie stood silently with her head down, her hair fallen across her face. Like her husband, she was overweight, her thighs and upper arms thick as logs. She wore dark cotton sweat pants and an oversized gray sweatshirt, probably one of Frank's, which reached to the top of her thighs. Her dirty tennis shoes gaped open, laceless. Frank let go of her hand and curled a heavy arm over her shoulders.

"Sally's been with us a long time," Frank said. "We'll miss her." Annie cried openly, noisily, her head pressed against Frank's chest, her right hand on his shoulder. He looked down at the top of her head. "You want to say anything, hon?" he asked her. Annie shook her head and burst into wild sobbing, sniffling and exhaling into Frank's shirt. Frank nodded at David. David picked up his shovel, scooped up dirt and stones, let them fall gently over the dog's body. He did this several times, then reached across the pile and began pulling the dirt and gravel into the hole. Slowly, Sally disappeared. David worked carefully, silently. He glanced up at his house and saw Janine standing in the window, still watching him.

When David finished, Frank lifted large pieces of sod he'd cut away and returned them over the bare earth, walked on them to press the roots of the grass into the loose, wet soil. Annie stood silently, her head down.

"Thank you," Frank said, reaching to shake David's hand. "All this mess in the middle of the night for a dog." He looked up at David's house. David was certain Frank saw Janine in the window, but Frank didn't acknowledge her. Frank shrugged his shoulders.

"Well. Good luck," he said.

"Thanks," David answered.

And then Frank did something David didn't expect. He crouched behind his wife, bent over and put one of his arms behind Annie's legs, the other along her back. With a loud grunt he picked her up. He lifted his wife to his chest, struggled a bit with the weight, then arched his back and stood tall. One of her shoes fell off, but they left it on the grass. Annie curled one arm around the back of Frank's neck and pressed her head under his chin. Awkwardly, Frank staggered toward the house, his wife in his arms. David watched them until they disappeared inside.

David grabbed his shovel and Frank's shovel and headed for home. His bedroom light was still on, but Janine no longer stood in the window. He pushed through the hedge into his own yard. The kitchen light shone. Through the lace curtains, he could see Janine sitting at the kitchen table.

David entered the house through the back door, kicked off his muddy slippers, climbed the few stairs that led from the entry into the kitchen.

"Janine," he said, "what are you doing up?"

She ignored his question. "What were you doing over at Frank and Annie's at this hour?" she asked.

"Their dog died," David said.

"Sally?" Janine asked.

David nodded. "Frank needed some help burying her."

"How awful," said Janine. "Poor Sally. What happened?"

"They had to put her down," David said. "They were pretty broken up about it. Frank didn't want the kids to see her that way."

David removed his jacket and hung it over the back of one of the vacant kitchen chairs. Janine glanced at him briefly but didn't meet his eyes. She didn't make an effort to stand up. "How did golf go tonight?" she asked.

David looked at Janine then, let his eyes focus intently on her face. She stared at some blank space at the other side of the table, refusing to look at him, the muscles in her face twitching. Her eyes glistened in the harsh kitchen light. Seeing her this way, David realized that she knew about Amy, had likely known for some time. She had simply been waiting. This recognition made his throat tighten. He gripped the back of the chair, spoke carefully, measuring his words.

"I did all right," he answered. "Nothing special."

"No?" Janine asked.

"I shot a ninety-two," David said. "I've done better."

"You got your money's worth," Janine said. "Isn't that what you usually say when you play poorly? You take more swings, so you say you got your money's worth."

"That's right," David said. "That's what I usually say."

Janine nodded. She looked up at him, finally. Tears that had welled up in her eyes spilled over, and she quickly wiped her face with her fingertips. "Oh my God," Janine said, her fingers beginning to shake.

"Janine, I'm sorry—" David began.

"Don't!" Janine said. She raised a hand at him, let it drop to the table.

In the agonizing silence that followed, David's mouth went dry. His legs grew weak. This is what it comes to, David thought, fearfully. This is the night we will always remember.

Janine clenched her teeth together, lowered her forehead into one hand, her elbow propped against the table. "I can't believe this is happening," she hissed. David's throat ached. He felt shocked by the sudden force of his own grief. He felt as if he might fall down. He tugged back on the chair, angled a hip into it, sat down across from Janine.

David looked down at his hands. Mud stained them, the creases also dark with Sally's blood. He clenched them into fists. He had no idea what to say, wondered how he would explain himself, what might come from his mouth. He thought wistfully, painfully, of Amy. He thought of the wonder of her body and spirit, the beauty of her face, her laughter, her wisdom, all particles, now, of the expanding universe, streaming away from him. David had been called upon to enact adultery's only law, as Amy knew he would be, his failures transparent all along, he realized now, to both wife and lover.

"Janine," David said. "Maybe *we* should get a dog. A puppy."

A small, disbelieving cry fell from Janine's mouth, but she bit her lip, stifled it. Above them, the kitchen light burned, the fluorescent tubes humming, shouldering back the darkness. David looked over her shoulder out the window, past the porch light, the neighbors' porch lights, the streetlights, stared into the millions of stars powdering the night sky. His heart burned. What he wanted to say was that every day while they were in Paris, he had gone alone, at noon, to stand in the square at place du Clovis. There he had closed his eyes and listened to the thundering bell of Notre-Dame. The music of the tolling bell had filled the cage of his ribs, had lifted him, made him lose his balance, stagger like someone drunk. It was as if his soul were being called from his body, the elements of his earthly life streaming back into space. What he wanted to say was that even though gravity binds us, love should pull us off our feet, carry us beyond our own borders, leave us weightless, intoxicated, gasping for air.

Adrienne's
Perfection

Cisco's sister, Adrienne, sometimes pushed back the cuticles of her fingernails with a butter knife until they bled. In the eighth grade, after learning the contents of hot dogs and sausages in science class, she quit eating meat. And she drained the hot water tank every time she took a shower. These traits were, in Cisco's view, Adrienne's only flaws. In every other way, Adrienne was perfect.

If she had been more normal—less beautiful, less athletic, less intelligent—Cisco's life might have been unbearable. Sibling rivalry would have consumed him. But because Adrienne lived so far beyond Cisco in all measurable categories, any comparisons between them seemed inappropriate, even absurd. No one ever thought to say, "Why can't you be more like your older sister?" because it would have been like asking Fritos to be more like a moon launching. So Cisco lived his life as the scrub brother of a perfect sister with daring and aplomb. Adrienne's perfection had freed him of all expectations.

Cisco's father, whom they called R&D (short for Responsibility and Discipline), and whom they hardly ever saw, seemed the lone dissenter in Cisco's effort to live life expectation-free. R&D owned a financial services company, and though he worked long hours and was rarely home, Cisco and Adrienne still avoided him whenever possible. Once Cisco had successfully gone a record eleven days straight without seeing or speaking to him. Cisco felt his father didn't so much have conversations as issue edicts and give speeches.

In front of friends or neighbors, R&D sometimes referred to Cisco and Adrienne as Oil and Water. Pure and drinkable, Adrienne, at seventeen, received the best of the family's genes bundled in a smart, gorgeous package: straight A's in school; a lithe, muscular body senior boys couldn't stop talking about; and stardom in athletics, particularly volleyball, at which she excelled. Cisco—his given name was Charlie but since a child he'd been Cisco, who knew why—was Oil, the genetic lottery loser. He made bad grades, suffered from terrible skin, and had muscle tone the consistency of yogurt. He hung out with other skateboarders and computer-game geeks, misfits like him who pierced their bodies in unusual places and dyed their hair in colors not found in nature.

Cisco and Adrienne's teachers did occasionally struggle with this discrepancy. After a year of being dazzled by Adrienne, they'd see Cisco amble into their classrooms, his hair shellacked into fuchsia spikes, his nose pierced, his baggy AF shorts hanging off his ass, and they'd double-check the name on their rosters. His geometry teacher, Mr. Dykehardt, who was also Adrienne's volleyball coach, had been the most brutal. "She's a champion," he'd whisper in Cisco's ear, during after-school detentions, "and you're a world-champion fuck-up." While other kids pretended to mispronounce Mr. Dykehardt's name, softening the first vowel and dropping the final "t," Cisco called him Hard On, or, when he was especially angry, Dick Head. Sophomore year, detentions had been a way of life.

Cisco had liked his French class—his only A, which saved him from the gulag of summer school—and his French teacher,

Mr. Dornacher, who would sometimes defy the school's fire code by cooking peanut butter and jelly crepes on a hot plate for his students while they discussed *The Little Prince* or *The Stranger,* books Cisco had found intriguing. Both of the writers, Saint-Exupery and Camus, had died tragically, Camus perhaps a suicide, which Cisco found made their books more meaningful. He also loved the fact that the French had elevated cigarette smoking to a virtue.

"Unlike Americans," Mr. Dornacher pointed out, disdainfully, "who make smoking a crime under the pretense of public health but eat like pigs at every meal, then have the gall to sue McDonald's when they become obese."

When he didn't have a detention with Dr. Dykehardt, Cisco would sometimes hang out in Mr. Dornacher's room after school, paging through old copies of *Paris Match,* looking for pictures of topless French women on St. Tropez beaches, while Mr. Dornacher graded tests. Near the end of the school year, Mr. Dornacher had said to Cisco, "Your sister Adrienne seems so sad. Why is that?"

"She does?"

"To me she does," he said. "Is everything all right at home?"

Cisco thought about it. "Well," he said. "My dad's an asshole."

Mr. Dornacher shrugged. "Anything else?"

Cisco laughed. "Isn't that enough?" he said.

Mr. Dornacher said, "When I play Edith Piaf in class, Adrienne cries."

"You said everyone in France cries when 'The Little Sparrow' sings."

"Yes. I was exaggerating, Cisco," Mr. Dornacher said. "For effect."

Cisco raised his eyebrows. "I like teachers who lie to their students. It makes learning more challenging."

But as summer began, Cisco believed Mr. Dornacher might have been right about Adrienne. She did seem sad. Cisco bubbled over with the joy of June emancipation, but Adrienne didn't seem to find pleasure in anything. Three or four days a week they'd drive to the pool together and spend the afternoon, apart, of course, with their separate circles of friends, but Adrienne would just lay on a towel with her sunglasses on, listening to music. Boys would come by, and she'd ignore them. To cool off, her friends would dive in off the diving board, tugging on their bikini bottoms as they climbed the ladder out of the pool, but Adrienne, who had once loved to swim, never got into the water.

Watching Adrienne at the pool, Cisco realized he didn't know her. They shared a bathroom, the whole second floor of their parents' sprawling house, for that matter, but they might just as well have been living on separate planets. Adrienne was The Stranger. About once a month Cisco would discover the bathroom wastebasket filled with wads of toilet tissue, blood sometimes oozing out of the bundles and drying brown. He'd occasionally snoop through Adrienne's bathroom products, body gels and facial masks, shampoos and conditioners, testing himself by reading the directions written in French and English on the back of the bottles. Sometimes he smelled the pungent scent of acetone wafting under her bedroom door when she removed old nail polish and replaced it with a new color. And he'd hear her voice on the telephone through her closed and locked bedroom door, talking to friends or one of the many boys who called her, always the popular ones, the master-race types with blue eyes and blonde hair, who drove hot cars and sometimes badgered Cisco in the school hallways in an effort to get the inside track down Adrienne's pants.

"Hey freak," Ricky Bass, the football team's muscular running back, had said, that last week of school, pinning Cisco to a locker with a hand against his sternum. "What's with Adrienne?"

"What do you mean?"

"Why won't she go out with me anymore?"

Cisco weighed several clever answers in his head, measuring the pleasure they'd give in delivery against the potential retaliatory pain they might cause.

"Dude," Cisco said, "she's not into that whole gender ambiguity thing you've got going."

"What the fuck are you talking about?"

"Hey, some girls love it—a sensitive guy who's confused about which way his fence gate is swinging. Adrienne's not like that. Don't get me wrong—she's not prejudiced. We went to Key West last year on vacation and she got to be pretty good friends with some of our gay waiters."

"I'm not a faggot, asshole," Ricky said, drilling Cisco's sternum with an index finger. "What the fuck are you talking about?"

Cisco raised his arms. "Dude, I'm just the messenger," Cisco said. "I hate rumors. They're so unfair."

"I'm not a switch hitter, either," Ricky said. "I'll kill whoever said that shit."

Cisco shrugged. "I believe you, man," he said, in a tone meant to convey doubt. Ricky stormed away.

About the second week of summer vacation, Mr. Dykehardt stopped by the house to drop off the paper work for an August volleyball camp at Purdue University—all the best prep players from all over the country would be there, Division I coaches, potential scholarships, blah, blah, blah. When Cisco opened the door and found Mr. Dykehardt standing helplessly on the porch, like a shy scout selling cookies, Cisco rejoiced. The glory of summer had put him out of reach.

"Hey Dick Head!" Cisco said, smiling.

"Hello Cisco," Mr. Dykehardt replied. "How's your summer going?"

Cisco smirked. "I'm getting high every day."

"Well, great. Perhaps you'll exceed my expectations and make it to prison even before you turn eighteen."

"That's me," Cisco said, "Mr. High Achiever."

"Is Adrienne at home? I need to speak to her about volleyball camp."

Cisco shook his head. "Didn't anybody tell you? Adrienne got in a car wreck last night. She's in the hospital, paralyzed from the neck down. Terrible tragedy."

Mr. Dykehardt frowned. "Just get your goddamn sister for me."

"What's the magic word?" Cisco asked.

Mr. Dykehardt took a deep breath and exhaled angrily. "Please."

Cisco grinned. "That was the magic word yesterday."

"Listen, punk," Mr. Dykehardt began, but Cisco cut him off.

"Adrienne!" he shouted up the stairs, over his shoulder. "Dick Head is here!"

Adrienne ran down the stairs and rolled her eyes at Cisco. She went out on the porch with Mr. Dykehardt and closed the door behind her. A few minutes later, she came back inside with the papers. Cisco sat on the steps, waiting.

"You going to volleyball camp?" Cisco asked.

"I don't know," Adrienne said. She looked as if she might cry.

"Don't let Hard On pressure you, man," Cisco said. "Take the summer off, Adrienne. Purdue University is in Indiana, isn't it? Who the fuck wants to go to Indiana in the summertime? Or anytime, for that matter?"

Adrienne smiled. "You don't understand," she said. "There's a lot of pressure."

Cisco feigned indignation. "Pressure? I don't understand pressure? Every time I had a geometry test last year, I took it without reading the chapter. That's pressure, Adrienne."

"And you flunked geometry."

"Did not," Cisco said. "I got a fucking D."

Adrienne laughed.

Encouraged, Cisco said, "Let's get high and go to the pool."

"I don't do drugs," Adrienne said.

"You're such a priss, Adrienne. You should smoke some weed. It will help you relax."

"Mom!" Adrienne yelled. "We're going to the pool!"

"Okay, dear," their mother answered, from somewhere deep inside the house. Their mother was an old-fashioned stay-at-home mom who took Valium, tiny little pills with V's carved into them. Very '70s, Cisco thought.

"You better be careful," Adrienne said. "Marijuana deforms your sperm."

"My sperm are fine," Cisco said. "I just saw them last week. They were wearing little white tuxedos."

"You look at them under a microscope?"

"Don't get gross, Adrienne."

Adrienne drove them to the pool. They had the top down on the Sebring convertible they shared and Linkin Park cranked on the stereo. The sun felt hot on Cisco's neck. He smiled. He loved the pool, the glimmer of the water, all those girls' glistening, barely dressed bodies, the smell of coconut oil, the cute lifeguards sitting like queen bees up on their white wooden thrones with their legs apart. Man, that summer feeling, Cisco thought.

When they pulled into the parking lot, Cisco turned off the stereo and ejected the CD, returned it to its case, and locked it in the glove box. He looked over at Adrienne. She was slumped over the steering wheel, crying.

"Come on, Adrienne," he said. "It's summer. Fuck volleyball camp. Have some fun."

She shook her head. "Maybe I should just go back home."

"What? Are you crazy!" He tugged on her arm. "Come on, let's go party!"

Adrienne wiped her eyes with her fingers. "All right," she said. "You go ahead. I've got to get my suit on."

"Let's stay until closing."

"Why?"

"You want to be there when R&D gets home from work?"

"It's his golf night," Adrienne said. "He won't be home until late."

"Oh, yeah. Sweet," Cisco said. "But still. Let's stay."

Adrienne sighed.

"Please?"

"Oh all right," she said.

Cisco left the car and headed for the water. Eventually, he saw Adrienne come through the gate. She carried her bag over to where her friends were laying out on the grass. She put a towel down. She sunned herself on her stomach, then on her back, rotating all afternoon like meat on a rotisserie. Her belly button was pierced and she wore a shiny red stone in her navel that matched her bikini. He had once told her it looked like a little piece of molten lava inside a volcano. A few boys came by, crouched down by her head, shading her face from the sun while they talked. Ricky Bass went by more than once, his muscles rippling. Cisco smiled each time Ricky walked away looking angry.

No dad, no teachers, no homework, a few hits of weed in the boys' bathroom with his buddies. Cisco smiled and floated through the afternoon.

Adrienne let Cisco drive on the way home. Since he only had his temporary learner's permit, and Adrienne wasn't yet eighteen, Cisco wasn't legally allowed to drive. And Adrienne never let him. But she gave him the keys and got in on the passenger side. It was after eight o'clock. The sun had started its free fall into the branches of nearby maple trees. Cisco and Adrienne were barely out of the parking lot when she began crying again. She put her face into her hands and sobbed, her sides heaving, her ribs swelling against her skin as if she were inflating and deflating herself.

"Hey, it'll be all right," Cisco said.

She shook her head. "It's not all right," Adrienne said.

"It's just fucking volleyball," Cisco said.

"No!" Adrienne said, angrily. Her voice came through her hair. "Stop the car, Cisco. Right now."

Cisco pulled over against the curb and shifted the car into park.

"You sound like R&D," Cisco said.

"Put the top up," she said.

"Yes sir," said Cisco. He pushed the button and the convertible top unfolded forward on its steel ribbing. The inside of the car darkened. "All right. Now what, captain?" he said.

Adrienne sniffled, pulled a tissue from her purse and wiped her nose. She blinked her eyes and looked down at her feet. "This has nothing to do with volleyball camp."

"It's not about volleyball camp."

"No."

"All right. I believe you. So what's the problem?"

"I'm in trouble," she said.

Cisco stifled a chuckle. "What kind of trouble?"

"*In trouble*," Adrienne repeated, enunciating each syllable. Cisco raised his eyebrows, listened for more. "I'm pregnant," Adrienne said, finally.

"What?" Cisco stared at Adrienne, his eyes falling to her stomach. "I don't believe you."

"I think I would know," Adrienne said.

"You don't even have a fucking boyfriend, Adrienne."

Adrienne shook her head. Her eyes watered and dripped tears.

She tried to speak but nothing came out of her mouth, and she began crying again. Cisco thought about all the boys around Adrienne at the pool. Johnny Schumacher. Victor Fuentes. Blaine. Joe. Fucking Ricky Bass. Adrienne had been out with some of them. Ricky, most recently.

"Are you sure? Maybe you just skipped a month, you know? That happens to girl jocks sometimes, right?"

Adrienne shook her head. "I did three tests."

"Maybe they were wrong."

"I've been throwing up every morning," said Adrienne.

"That's what that noise is?"

"It's hard to puke quietly," Adrienne said. "I can't believe R&D hasn't said anything."

"If they hear you, I'm sure they think it's me. R&D was in my room last week looking for the key to the liquor cabinet."

"You don't even drink."

"I know! Alcohol is bad for you, man. Look at how fucked up Mom is."

"Mom's depressed."

"Mom drinks a pint of gin every day, Adrienne."

"Because she's depressed."

"Well, she should get off that retro shit and take Paxil or Prozac like everybody else."

Adrienne laughed and this made Cisco smile. "See," he said. "Life's not so bad."

"Speak for yourself."

"Adrienne, tell me this," Cisco said. "I don't mean anything bad by what I'm asking. But do you even know who the guy is?"

Adrienne rolled her eyes. "What does it matter?" Adrienne said.

"What does it matter? Jesus, Adrienne. Just tell me it wasn't that asshole muscle-head Ricky Bass. I couldn't take it."

"I'm not talking about that," Adrienne said.

"Just tell me it wasn't him," Cisco said. "That's all I'm asking."

"Just stop asking, all right? I told you I'm not talking about it. Are you going to help me or not?"

"You want my help?"

"Yes. I want your help."

"So what do you want me to do? Take ten of my friends to Ricky Bass's house so he can beat us all up?"

Adrienne shook her head. "I want to get an abortion."

"I can't do that! Shit, Adrienne."

"I don't want you to do it," she said. "I want you to take me to the clinic where I can have it done. I want you to drive me there."

Cisco nodded. More manageable, certainly. But still. "Wouldn't you want one of your friends do that?"

"I don't want anyone else to know," Adrienne said.

"No one else knows?"

"No," she answered. "No one."

Cisco shook his head. "Damn," he said. "Damn! All right. You know I'll do it."

"There's a place in Milwaukee. I have an appointment. Next Thursday. We'll have to go twice. Thursday and Friday. The first day they just do an exam and explain everything. Then the next day you go in and have it done."

"And you're sure you want to do this? I mean, there are other possibilities, right? Have you thought it all through?" It seemed a ridiculous question as soon as it passed his lips. Of course she had thought it through.

"Believe me," Adrienne said. "There are no other possibilities."

When they got home, both sides of the garage were blocked by two Saabs, a BMW, and Mrs. Davenport's new yellow Hummer. It was Mother's card party night.

"Look at that fucking Hummer," Cisco said. "How ugly is that? It's like a train car with rubber wheels. Who'd pay fifty K for that?"

"If Mrs. D drives drunk, she wants the upper hand in a crash."

"And who the fuck thought up that name?" Cisco asked. "Didn't they know hummer is slang for blow job?"

"It is?"

"You don't know that, Adrienne? How you can be pregnant when you don't even know what a fucking hummer is?"

"Shhhh!" Adrienne said, laughing.

"I'm serious!"

"Have you ever had one?"

"What? A hummer? Who's gonna do that to a freak like me with pink hair and zits all over his face?"

"Someone will. Someday," Adrienne said.

"Yeah, someday over the rainbow—like Dorothy and the Tin Man. You notice they hardly ever show Tin Man below the waist? My buddy Brock says it's because Tin Man has a permanent stiffy for Dorothy. All rusty, too."

"That's disgusting," Adrienne said.

"Brock told me this one: You know how Tin Man beats off?" Cisco asked.

"No."

"With a socket wrench."

Adrienne shook her head.

"Yeah, that's pretty lame," Cisco said.

Cisco pulled the car along the street in the front yard, careful to avoid going too far on the grass, which would anger R&D. The lawn service used enough herbicide on his father's perfect, golf-green lawn to kill every weed in the whole county. Cisco and Adrienne crossed the lawn toward the house. The windows were open, and they could hear voices and laughter coming from the kitchen.

Inside, cigarette smoke swirled in the smoky light and all five women drank gin or vodka from martini glasses. The open bottles stood like sentries on the kitchen island. Next to them, green olives floated in a jar the size of a basketball.

"There are my babies!" Mother said, throwing an arm around Cisco's neck, then Adrienne's. They each bent for a kiss on the cheek. Her breath smelled like pine trees. Cisco went around the table and kissed all of the other women, smelling their lipstick and perfume, and they all smiled and laughed and made small talk, asked him if he had a girlfriend, a summer job, someone who regularly did his hair like that. No to everything.

"And what do you think of my new Hummer?" Mrs. Davenport asked him. Cisco glanced at Adrienne and then looked down at the back of Mrs. D's leathery, sun-tanned neck. One could often be a little more honest with drunks, because sometimes so much time passed between what you said and when it nestled into their brain that it failed to make sense to them—sort of like kicking a dinosaur on the tail. But Cisco didn't want to chance it. He was close to getting out of the room without being asked anything too embarrassing or overhearing more than he wanted to hear. One time he overheard Mrs. D telling Mrs. Gardiner that she had her bird nest waxed every other week through the summer bikini season. "Smooth as a baby's bottom," she'd said, winking. "Henry"—that was Mrs.D's younger second husband—"loves it." Sometimes one could know too much.

"I'd love to get one of those," Cisco said.

Mrs. D. nodded. "Honey, if Martha Stewart gives me a hot tip on my ImClone stock, and it triples, I'll give you one myself." All the women laughed.

"That's great Mrs. D," Cisco said. He smirked at Adrienne and made his exit as she began her obligatory tour of the table.

On Thursday morning, Cisco and Adrienne told their mother they were going to the pool and left Cedarburg to drive to the Summit Women's Health Center on Water Street in downtown Milwaukee. A few blocks from the house, Adrienne pulled the car over and they switched places, with Cisco behind the wheel.

Soon he was merging onto the interstate, pushing on the gas, setting the cruise on seventy-two, his first taste of that kind of speed on the open highway. Adrienne slouched in her seat and stared out the window. Cisco turned on the radio, gripped the smooth steering wheel in both hands, sang along to the songs he knew the whole thirty-minute drive. As they approached the city, the traffic thickened, the highway clogged with commuters. Cisco slowed down and settled into a slot in the bumper-to-bumper traffic.

"This sucks," he said, as they inched forwarded, surrounded by cars and concrete.

Adrienne nodded.

They finally exited downtown and Cisco parked the car on the fifth level of an eight-level concrete parking structure located just across the street from the Health Center. From street level and from above, the gray building that housed the clinic looked decrepit, with windows on multiple floors sporting vacancy signs.

Cisco and Adrienne locked the car and rode the elevator down to street level. When the elevator doors opened they were accosted immediately by three women chanting anti-abortion slogans and passing out anti-abortion literature. One of the women pressed a pamphlet about adoption into his hand, and another kept shouting at him that he was a deadbeat dad. "Don't do this," said another. "Don't kill your baby." The protesters walked quickly, stride for stride on each side of Cisco and Adrienne, their eyes wild.

"What the fuck is this?" Cisco said angrily. Adrienne began crying. She broke into a jog and crossed the street. Cisco ran beside her, and the women ran along next to them. Outside the clinic, an old woman with thinning gray hair stood at the door wearing a sandwich board with a huge picture of an aborted fetus on it. Cisco stared at the picture. The baby looked orange and wrinkled, curled like a boiled shrimp. "No!" the woman kept saying, over and over, while shaking her head. "No! No!"

Adrienne tugged the door open and they rushed inside. When the door closed behind them, they were left alone, in silence.

"What the hell was that?" Cisco asked.

Adrienne hung her head and shook it. She wiped the tears from her face. They climbed a dark, narrow staircase, opened another door, and entered a room lit by overhead fluorescent lights, a doctor's office waiting room, with wooden chairs arranged in rows, and wrinkled magazines strewn on various tables and empty chairs. On a table in the middle of the room was a three-dimensional plastic sculpture of a woman's reproductive organs. The uterus looked like a red light bulb. The ovaries and fallopian tubes reminded Cisco of the seed pods that emerged after his mother's poppies bloomed. About a dozen other young women sat quietly around the room, not reading, not talking, just waiting. Only one of them was with a boyfriend, and she sat with her head on his shoulder, crying, as he stared at the ceiling, looking embarrassed. He made brief eye contact with Cisco and then returned his gaze to the ceiling tiles. Adrienne walked to the counter where a nurse sat behind a sliding glass window. The nurse nodded, and Adrienne walked back to join Cisco.

He picked through the magazines, couldn't find anything he liked, so paged his way through a copy of *Glamour*. Adrienne sat next to him, her arms crossed, her eyes closed.

After about an hour, a nurse called Adrienne. Adrienne stood up, then reached down and grabbed Cisco's wrist.

Cisco looked up at her. Adrienne nodded.

They were lead into an examining room where another nurse was waiting. All business, she asked Adrienne to lie down on the table, pull up her shirt, and slide her underpants down off her hips. Adrienne did as she was told. Cisco averted his eyes. The nurse put green gel on the head of the ultrasound wand, told Adrienne it would be cold, then pressed it to her belly. She asked Adrienne how far along she thought she was.

"Seven or eight weeks," Adrienne said.

The nurse rubbed the ultrasound head on Adrienne's belly for about ten seconds, making small circles in the area just beneath the silver ring in Adrienne's pierced navel. As she did so, the nurse watched the computer screen intently. Then she stopped. "Okay," she said. "We're done. Looks like seven or eight weeks."

"Can you tell what it is?" Adrienne asked.

The nurse smiled. "Of course not," she said.

They were sent back into the waiting room, and about fifteen minutes later they were summoned again, this time to see Dr. Mulroy, a tall, middle-aged black man with graying hair, wearing a white lab coat with his name embroidered in light green over one pocket. He introduced himself, shook their hands, then led them into a tiny, carpeted office. He sat down behind a small desk, and Cisco and Adrienne sat in chairs across the desk. Cisco had to tip his chair forward to get the office door closed. An old computer rested on the desk amid unkempt stacks of papers and, over Dr. Mulroy's shoulder, Cisco could recognize a diploma of some kind thumbtacked to the paneled wall.

Dr. Mulroy gave Adrienne a form to fill out and sign, stipulating that he had discussed with her everything on the form, which he hadn't, of course. He said the State of Wisconsin required that he meet with every patient and discuss every option twenty-four hours before performing the actual procedure. He'd been doing this for twenty-one years, he said.

Adrienne nodded. She signed the form and passed it back across the desk. Tears spilled down her cheeks.

Dr. Mulroy held up his closed fist to imitate a woman's cervix, pointed to places where he'd inject a local anaesthetic to numb the pain of dilating the cervix, which he said was the most painful part of the procedure. There'd be a gentle suction for about five minutes—he held up a small, clear plastic tube—and then the pregnancy would be gone. Adrienne would feel some cramping both during and after, and in the recovery room they'd provide ice packs and pain relievers. He'd send her home with a prescription for painkillers and antibiotics.

Adrienne's shoulders started shaking as she cried. Dr. Mulroy leaned forward in his chair and reached across his desk.

"You're having a hard time with this, I can tell," he said. "Is this your first one?"

Adrienne nodded.

"Really? Your first one. Well, my advice to you," he said, "is have a good cry, and then put it behind you." He fell back into his chair and motioned with his arms. "Just put it behind you." He waved an arm toward the little window. "Those people out there aren't interested in helping anyone. Abortion isn't tragic. What's tragic is young women having babies and then suffocating them, or leaving them in a dumpster somewhere. Where are the protesters then? What are they doing for those young women?" Dr. Mulroy had a soft, confident way of speaking. Cisco knew that he couldn't have been a very good doctor to be spending his career in a cramped office inside a crumbling building with a For Sale sign in the front window. But it pleased him to see the doctor treat Adrienne so kindly.

When the appointment was over, they descended the stairs and opened the door, breaking immediately into a run as the anti-abortion women tried to encircle them. They cut through traffic on Water Street and entered the parking structure. One of the women stayed with them, stood with them as they waited for the elevator. Cisco put his arm around Adrienne, shielded her as best he could as the woman waved literature in their faces and told them not to make this mistake. "Don't do this," she said. "You'll regret it for the rest of your life." The elevator door opened and they got in. As the doors closed, the woman shouted, "Don't despair. Don't despair." The elevator lurched upward. Cisco could feel Adrienne crying.

They found the car, wove their way through the spiraling concrete tunnel to the exit gate, then found their way back to the freeway. Cisco finally relaxed when they hit the interstate. He merged into traffic, turned on the A/C, set the cruise at 72. He looked over at Adrienne. She sat slouched in the seat, her knees up on the dash, her eyes closed.

"That went well," he said to her. She glanced at him, then closed her eyes again.

Cisco popped a CD in the stereo, Boston's debut album, music R&D used to listen to back in college. Buzzing guitars and a steady beat, lyrics that made you feel alive. Hard to imagine R&D ever listening to this, he thought.

Soon they left the traffic and tall buildings of Milwaukee and were cruising toward the trees and open meadows of the suburbs.

Fifteen minutes into the drive home, Adrienne sat up in her seat. She leaned forward and turned off the stereo.

"Hey, I like that shit!" Cisco said, protesting.

"I have to tell you something," Adrienne said. "Something I promised never to tell."

"Maybe you shouldn't," Cisco said.

Adrienne shook her head. "I want to," she said.

"All right," Cisco said. "So what is it?"

Adrienne turned toward him in the seat. She put her hands on the seat between them. "You have to promise never to repeat this."

"Like you promised," he said.

"Yes," she said. "Only you can't ever tell anyone else."

"All right," Cisco said. "I promise."

Adrienne took a deep breath. "I'm not really your sister," she said. "I'm your half-sister."

"What?" Cisco said. "Half what?"

"It means we have the same mom," Adrienne said. "But I have a different father than you do."

"R&D isn't your dad?" Cisco asked.

Adrienne shook her head. "Not my biological father, no."

"That's fucking ridiculous."

"No," she said. "It's the truth."

"I don't believe you."

"It's true, Cisco," Adrienne said.

"How do you know?"

"Mom told me," she said.

"No way!"

Adrienne nodded. "When I was thirteen. I'd just started bleeding and she gave me the sex talk. Men are as persistent as the sun, she said. You will feel their heat, you will want them inside you. But you have to be smart. And then she told me. Not long after she married R&D, she had an affair with a married man, a man she loved more than her own life, a man she would have died for. When she got pregnant, he refused to see her again. It almost killed her, she said."

"Man," Cisco said, his mind racing. "I can't believe this."

"That other man is my father."

"Jesus, Adrienne. I can't fucking believe it. Does R&D know?"

"No," Adrienne said. "No way."

"Did you ever meet the guy?"

"My biological dad?" Adrienne asked. "Never. But Mom has a picture of him. I've seen it."

"What did he look like?"

Adrienne shrugged. "A little like me," I guess, she said. "Only a man, obviously."

"Damn," Cisco said, shaking his head. "No wonder Mom's so messed up."

"You can't tell anyone," Adrienne said. "Ever."

Cisco nodded. "I won't," he said. "Christ. I won't."

Adrienne turned away from him. She looked out the window. Cisco didn't turn the music back on. He kept thinking about Adrienne's revelation, kept glancing over at Adrienne, looking at her nose, at her shoulders, at the slight curl in her hair. Only half of her was made of the same stuff he was. No wonder, he thought. No wonder.

He noticed Adrienne looking at him again. She stared at him. Through the corner of his eye, Cisco could see her watching him with persistence.

"What now?" he asked.

"How fast can this car go?" she asked.

"I don't know," Cisco said. "It's got a V8 in it. A hundred, maybe. I have no idea."

"One hundred's fast, isn't it?"

Cisco smiled. "Hell yes," he said.

"So try it. See how fast this car can go."

Cisco glanced at her. "Why?"

"We could just open the windows and drive. It would be like flying."

Cisco gripped the wheel and swallowed. "We might blow a tire," he cautioned.

Adrienne laughed. "I don't care," she said. "We should just turn the music up as loud as it goes and drive, Cisco. Just drive and not ever go back home. And when it feels right, when it seems as if everything is perfect, you can steer the car into one of those concrete pillars that hold up the bridges. Going a hundred and ten, or a hundred and twenty, when we hit that concrete, we'd just pass instantly into whatever next world is waiting. Nothing would be left of us."

Cisco looked at Adrienne. Her eyes were locked on his. He tried to swallow again. His mouth had suddenly gone dry. "You want to Thelma and Louise it?" Cisco asked. "Is that what you're fucking saying?"

Adrienne stared at him and nodded.

"Are you fucking around with me?" Cisco asked.

Adrienne shook her head. Her eyes glassed over with tears. "I know you've thought about it," she said.

Cisco shook his head, but it was true. At various moments in his life, when R&D was riding his ass about one thing or another, when their mother was sloshing around the living room knocking over lamps, and he just felt like shit, felt like nothing mattered, nothing would ever matter, he'd let himself think about dying, about the instant peace of it. In his darkest moments, it was true, the thought of dying held some comforting light. When he was fourteen, his brain in a dark hole with high walls, and R&D had hit him, had slapped him for coloring his hair, getting his nose pierced, he'd spent a few furious days buying Ecstasy from various friends who had older brothers and sisters in college. He had accumulated nearly a dozen pills. Though his despair remained, over time, his anger had weakened. R&D had slipped him a twenty as he left the house one night to go to the skate park with some of his buddies, war reparations, perhaps, or a feeble effort to buy love. Cisco took the money, felt bought off, pissed off. He and his buddies each dropped a pill, rode the half-pipe until four in the morning. He never fell asleep that night. The next morning, feeling like total shit, he flushed the rest of the Ecstasy down the toilet.

Cisco broke into a sweat. "I don't know, Adrienne," he said.

"What's not to know?" she asked.

He shook his head. "I don't think I could do it."

"Please," she said. "*Please.*"

"A hundred miles an hour *would* be fucking wild," he said. He felt the gas pedal under his foot.

Adrienne nodded.

Cisco's thighs started shaking. "Let's see how eighty-five feels," Cisco said. He turned off the cruise and hit the gas. The car responded powerfully, and the red needle climbed to eighty, then to eighty-five. Adrienne cut off the A/C and lowered her window. A hard, noisy wind buffeted them. Cisco had to turn his face away from it to breathe. Adrienne pushed the Boston CD back into the stereo and turned the volume up until his ears rattled. Cisco could feel the bass guitar thumping against his chest. He tipped his head back and howled, but could barely hear himself. His heart pounded and his stomach felt on fire.

Adrienne suddenly pulled off her seat belt and slid over next to him. She jammed her left foot over the top of his, pressing down harder on the accelerator. The car lurched forward again. The needle ticked over ninety and Cisco had to swerve around a car ahead of them in the left lane. He looked in the rear view mirror to see a man's fist shaking out an open window. Another car loomed ahead of them, and Cisco merged right again, passed the car, and then merged left. The car leaned and bobbed as he turned, the tires squealing.

"Holy shit!" Cisco screamed.

He glanced down at the speedometer. Ninety-five. Adrienne kissed him on the cheek.

Cisco pushed the accelerator all the way to the floor. He glanced at his hands. His knuckles were white. He gripped the wheel so tightly his palms were cramping. Outside the car, the world passed in a blur. Cars, road signs, telephone poles, corn fields. They were speed and sound. Adrenaline flooded his muscles.

They passed a State Patrol car in the median, and Cisco's stomach fell. He couldn't tell if a radar gun was pointed at them or not, but at their speed, it didn't really matter. The red lights came on before they'd even passed the car, and the cop pulled out behind them and accelerated.

"Don't stop!" Adrienne shouted.

She turned on her knees and looked out the back window. Cisco panicked. He let off on the gas. The car slowed to about eighty. He looked in the rearview. The cop's headlights were flashing, strobe-like, and the cherries on top whirled brightly. He turned the stereo down and could hear the faint whine of the police siren.

"That's a *Crown Vic*," Cisco said. "We can't outrun that, Adrienne."

"We don't have to," Adrienne said.

Cisco slowed to seventy, then fifty-five. "Please don't stop, Cisco," Adrienne said. The cop followed closely behind them now, his front bumper seemingly just inches away from them. "I'm sorry, Adrienne," Cisco said. His hands shook. Fear filled his chest cavity, making it almost impossible to breathe. At the next exit, he pulled off the freeway and stopped on the ramp. Adrienne would not look at him. Her lower lip quivered as she fought tears. One cop was already at the window, hand on his holster, his partner crouching on the other side of the car. On the bridge in front of them, Cisco could see another police car coming toward them, lights flashing, siren screaming. Life got more difficult.

When Adrienne's best friend, Sylvia, came to the house the next morning to take Adrienne to the pool for the day, Cisco knew they were driving to Milwaukee. He sat alone in his room, his learner's permit gone, court dates looming in his future, his whole summer pretty much shot, and yet he felt he had betrayed Adrienne, had been called upon for help and had let her down. All day he waited for Sylvia to bring his sister home, and that finally happened, about four o'clock. He heard a car in the driveway and looked out his bedroom window. He watched Sylvia help Adrienne get out. Sylvia held Adrienne's elbow as she walked up the sidewalk to the house. He opened his bedroom door to listen as they came into the house.

Sylvia told their mother that Adrienne had gotten sick at the pool, some bad nachos, or something, Sylvia said, and he stood back and closed his door as Adrienne and Sylvia slowly ascended the stairs. He heard the two of them go into Adrienne's bedroom and close the door. About twenty minutes later, Sylvia left.

Twice Cisco walked across the hallway, put his hand on the doorknob, but he didn't go in.

In the morning, he heard Adrienne go into the bathroom, heard the shower run for a half-hour, then listened as the bathroom door opened again. There was a knock on his door. He opened it. Adrienne. She turned and walked into her room. Cisco followed.

Adrienne got into bed still wearing her bathrobe and pulled the covers up to her chest. Cisco closed the door behind them. The room was meticulously clean, painted pale yellow. Her bookshelves were neatly organized, the books probably even alphabetized by title. A CD organizer stood next to her stereo, and her cell phone rested on the end table next to her. A computer hummed on her desk, the screensaver, a multi-colored ball, bouncing around in the cyberspace.

"How did it go?" Cisco asked.

Tears spilled from Adrienne's eyes and she shook her head.

"Does it hurt?" Cisco asked.

Adrienne shrugged. "I've got Vicodin."

"Can I have a couple?"

Adrienne shook her head. "Never share prescriptions." She managed a smirk. "It's dangerous."

Cisco sat down on the floor by her bed and crossed his legs. "I'm grounded for the summer. At hard labor."

"I'm sorry," said Adrienne. "I heard him shouting. I told him it was my idea, but he wouldn't believe me."

Cisco shrugged. "It was kind of fun seeing him so mad."

Adrienne sat up in her bed and slowly pulled her knees up to her chin. The pain made her wince.

Cisco said, "I told Brock about our little adventure with the State Patrol. I said we were going a hundred miles an hour." Cisco smiled. "He told everybody. I'm like a legend already, or something."

Adrienne shook her head. "I don't know what I was thinking."

"I do," said Cisco. "Believe me. I know." He looked down at his feet. An awkward silence expanded between them, and Cisco broke it. "R&D posted my jobs for the week on the fridge. I've got to mow the lawn, wash and wax the cars, and clean the windows on the house, all before Saturday."

"I'll help you," Adrienne said. "I'll do everything."

Cisco shook his head. "Don't worry about it. He'll run out of things eventually. The grass only grows so fast."

"I'm sorry," Adrienne said, again. She wiped her face with her hands, but as soon as she did so her body shook with her sobbing.

"I can't stop crying."

Cisco nodded. "Just do what that doctor said," Cisco said.
"Put it behind you, Adrienne. Just put it behind you and move on."

Adrienne shrugged. "I can't," she whimpered.

"I'll teach you," Cisco said. "Seriously. I've been putting shit behind me all my life. It's like riding a fucking bike. Once you figure it out, it's not so hard."

Adrienne nodded and wiped her nose with a clump of tissue.

"Hey, look at the bright side," Cisco said, getting back to his feet. "Now you can go to volleyball camp. How bad can Indiana be in the summer? No worse than here, right? At least R&D won't be around."

Adrienne looked at him with sad eyes. She reached toward him with her hand, touched him lightly on the arm. "Cisco," she said, sadly. "There is no volleyball camp. There never was a volleyball camp."

"What are you talking about?"

She looked down at her knees. "I think you can figure it out."

Cisco stared at his sister, but Adrienne refused to look at him. And then the tumblers all fell into place, and the lock clicked open. The muffled phone calls, the way Adrienne dismissed Ricky Bass and all of the other boys. The paper work for volleyball camp. Mr. Dykehardt. Married Mr. Dykehardt, who had daughters Cisco's age. Cisco's mouth fell open.

"Don't say anything," Adrienne pleaded.

"That is so sick!" Cisco said.

"Don't—"

"I should kill that asshole."

"Please stop it," said Adrienne.

"You are way better than him, Adrienne," Cisco said. "Way better."

"Please!" she said again. She pressed a finger to Cisco's lips and looked up at him. "Don't say anything else. Not now. Not ever.

That's over."

Cisco nodded. His brain swirled with questions—how, why, where—that would never be asked or answered. His anger sickened him, but as Adrienne's eyes held him softly, steadily, something else happened, too. He felt a sudden flush of excitement, some thrilling pulse of happiness or relief he couldn't name. He felt less isolated, as if he'd somehow just been pulled free of a difficult world he once believed had chosen him, had singled out him alone, for daily loss and shame.

ln s

tructional
Technologies

When Professor Butler keeled over, at first we all thought he was faking it. In the middle of his lecture, he suddenly staggered forward, clawing madly at his chest, as guttural, gurgling noises bubbled up his throat. A string of saliva swung from his lower lip. He collapsed across an empty desk, toppling it over, and dropped face-first to the floor.

A few students applauded.

We waited ten seconds or so for Professor Butler to stand up and re-sume his lecture, but someone noticed blood pooling beneath his face, a poppy-red bloom on the white tile, and a few women in the front row lifted their feet and started screaming. I thought maybe he'd really tricked us this time, that he had somehow slipped a capsule of food col-oring into his mouth to make his fall more realistic. But then we noticed the darkening of his pants, the spread of urine on the floor, and we figured even Professor Butler wouldn't have gone *that* far to make us pay attention in his class.

When the paramedics arrived, they rolled Dr. Butler to his back, his great belly rising like an empty beer barrel in a pool of water. His bulbous nose had been flattened to one side, and some of his blood had clotted in his silver mustache, which was tinged a brownish yellow from all the cigarettes he'd smoked in his life. One of his front teeth, broken in half, remained on the floor. It looked like a peppermint Chicklet.

They wheeled Professor Butler out of the classroom and loaded him into a waiting ambulance, and even then I thought perhaps he'd really fooled us all, that maybe he'd planned the whole, elaborate scheme. I wondered about that up until the following Wednesday when a substitute teacher and fly-fisherman named Professor Paine arrived with Dr. Butler's lecture notes and changed the course of my life.

By that summer, I had decided that I didn't want to become a teacher, but I was going through with it anyway. I'd been in college six years already, and when I tried to tell my father I was thinking about changing majors again, he popped his cork. He said, "William, when you're halfway over Niagara Falls bare-assed in a barrel, don't you think it's a bit late to change your mind?" Professor Butler's death gave me one final opportunity to get out of the barrel and sidestroke for shore, but I didn't take it. I stayed in the class. All of the students did, at first.

"Instructional Technologies" was required for all students seeking K-12 teaching certification. It was one of the last college courses I needed to finish my English Education major. The course met on Wednesday nights in the eight-week summer session from six to nine o'clock, and covered various technologies of instruction, such as how to use the chalkboard, overhead projectors, copy and ditto machines, VCRs, eight-millimeter movie projectors, and so forth. Frankly, it was a bullshit course. An easy A if you could just manage to stay awake, which was a challenge sometimes.

When he was still alive, Professor Butler did his best to keep us interested. He had taught "Instructional Technologies" for centuries, and he brought to it the zeal of a Pentecostal preacher, pacing and coughing and gesticulating wildly with his hands as he lectured: "Thumbtacks give you a nice, clean look, but once they're in it's like trying to draw the sword from the stone to get them back out again! It's like pulling spikes with your fingernails! Pushpins with fluorescent plastic caps are the wave of the future. And they're easy to see if you drop them. In my early career as a teacher, the bottom of my shoes were so full of tacks I sounded like a tap-dancer when I walked down the halls. Clickety, clickety, clickety, I sounded like a dog without his toenails trimmed!"

When this enthusiasm failed to capture our attention, Professor Butler turned to melodrama. Occasionally, he'd pretend to be schizophrenic and would have arguments with a second personality he called "Dr. Ruby Doobie," who would often break into song, bellowing a few off-key lines from *Oklahoma!* Sometimes he would drop to the floor and crawl around the classroom between the rows of desks, dragging his left leg. "I think I've had a stroke!" he would say. "But don't call an ambulance yet! We have a lesson plan to finish!" At other times he'd feign a heart attack, clutching his chest with both hands, holding his breath until his face flushed red and his eyes bulged, before falling forward over an empty desk to the floor.

But he wouldn't be doing that anymore.

"He yelled 'wolf' once too often, man," Matt Gombie, one of the students in class, said, "and it came back to bite him in the ass."

The subject on the syllabus of that first class period without Dr. Butler was entitled, "Chalk Talk: Using the Chalk Board Effectively." Professor Paine, a tall, balding, tired-looking man in his fifties, with puffs of curly hair above his ears and a mustache that grew completely over his mouth, read in a soft monotone from Dr. Butler's notes:

"Never lean against a chalkboard wearing a dark shirt or coat. . . . To avoid the annoying screech new chalk sometimes makes on a clean

chalkboard, soften the chalk by holding the tip in your mouth for
a few seconds or lick it occasionally while you write. . . . Clean erasers
by tumbling them for twenty minutes at home in your clothes dryer,
on the cool cycle. Remember to remove other clothing before doing
so." From time to time, he'd pause to shake his head at the material,
then drink from a can of Jolt that rested on a table beside the lectern.
He wore a rumpled shirt and tie and blue jeans, and when he unbut-
toned his sport coat, we discovered that his tie was shaped like a fish
hanging by its tail. A brown trout, it turned out. "Genus *Salmo trutta*,"
Professor Paine noted, enthusiastically, when someone inquired.
"The native trout of Europe. First stocked in North America in 1883.
A *majestic* fish! One of God's finer inspirations."

   An hour into the class, two students in the back row had fallen
asleep. Matt Gombie had drawn a naked girl on his desk in pencil,
with breasts the size of melons, and smiling faces where the nipples
should have been. Professor Paine suddenly stopped lecturing.
He looked distraught.

   "Dr. Butler was a good man," he said. "He believed in this course."
Professor Paine shuffled the lecture notes and returned them to the file.
"I, on the other hand, do not, even though it has fallen to me, as the
Associate Dean of the College of Education, to finish teaching it.
I cannot bear to read another word of this. Dr. Butler, rest his soul,
has three hours of lecture notes here on how to use the chalkboard.
Three hours! One wouldn't think that would be possible, but there it is.
I read you the first hour. We've all suffered quite enough." He tapped
the edge of the file on the lectern and sighed. "Class dismissed."

   The subject of class the next week was how to use a VCR. Fifteen
minutes into the class, Professor Paine had not yet arrived. While most
of us sat quietly pondering our uncertain futures, other students debat-

ed how long students were obliged to wait for tardy professors before leaving. They'd nearly reached a consensus of fifteen minutes when Professor Paine walked through the door, trailed by his eleven-year-old son, a skinny boy he introduced as Peter (" Peter Paine?" someone whispered, to earn a burst of laughter), who wore green rubber fishing waders that came to the top of his thighs. The freckle-faced boy spent the first fifteen minutes of class clomping around in his waders, explaining how to show a movie on the VCR and how to pre-program it to record television shows. He said he had taped every episode of Babe Winkleman's "Good Fishing." While Peter taught the class, Professor Paine sat on the table in front of the room, reading *Field & Stream*. He wore faded blue jeans, a blue t-shirt, and a fishing vest, the kind with a small cloud of fleece over one pocket.

"That's it," Professor Paine said, when the boy finished explaining things to us. "That's enough, Peter. Thank you." He looked at us. "Who *doesn't* understand how to program a VCR? Anyone? Anyone besides me, that is?"

No hands went up.

"Well!" he said. "Good! There you have it. We're done." He looked up at the clock. It was not yet six-thirty. "We still have some time left. The Hex hatch is on over at the White River. Right now, trophy brown trout are out there slurping mayflies the size of hummingbirds. Peter and I are going night fishing. Anyone care to join us?" No one moved.

Kyle Prentice leaned over and whispered, "This guy's crazier than Butler."

I smiled and nodded. This was true, but I liked Professor Paine. He was like a spark in a room full of gasoline cans. He had an aura about him of unrealized potential, something I recognized in myself.

"You?" he asked, pointing to me. "You nodded. You want to

go fishing?"

"Me?" I stammered. "Not tonight. No."

"Why not?"

"Well," I said, embarrassed, "I don't fish."

Kyle Prentice laughed.

"What's your name?" Professor Paine inquired.

"Bill," I said. "William Knight."

"Mr. Knight," Professor Paine said, "you live in central Wisconsin, surrounded by some of the finest brown trout streams in the Midwest, and you don't fish?"

"No," I said. "I don't." This was the truth. I had never fished in my life. My father didn't fish. His father didn't fish. I came from a line of men whose sole purpose in life was to make money, who were good at it, and who rejected any activity that distracted them from that end. Like Dr. Butler, my grandfather had died working, while sitting in his leather chair at the bank. My father had inherited that chair. I did not intend to sit there.

Professor Paine shook his head sadly and left. His son followed him out of the room, the sound of his thumping waders fading in the distance down the hallway.

"Cool!" said Matt Gombie, who popped out of his desk. "Time to party, dudes!" he said, and left the room. The rest of us milled around like sheep left in a pen after slaughter, pondering what to make of our good fortune.

"This is ridiculous," Sherry Warner said. "We're paying good money for this course, and he's not even teaching it." There's always some dizzy capitalist in every class who believes that educations are purchased like pork belly futures. "If this happens again," she added, "I'm calling the dean."

"He *is* the dean," Kyle Prentice said.

"No he's not," Sherry said, "he's the associate dean. The Dean of Education is Dr. Gladdens. I know him. He plays golf with my dad."

"Man, don't call Dr. Glad Bag," said Kyle. "Just let it be. You learned how to work a VCR didn't you? What's the problem?"

"The problem," Sherry said, "is that I paid for three hours and I only got fifteen minutes."

"Hey, the shit's on sale!" Kyle said. "Enjoy it!"

Professor Paine was in class waiting for us when we arrived the following week at six o'clock. He sat eating a Big Mac and reading *Fly Rod & Reel* magazine. He wore another of his fish ties, this one a rainbow trout, "genus *Salmo Gairdneri*," he'd written on the board, "native to North America. Migratory species are known as STEELHEAD. A GLORIOUS fish!" The chairs were arranged in a circle around a table which held a ditto machine. Next to it was a large, white Canon photocopier and a smaller machine used to make ditto masters.

When we were all there, Professor Paine started class.

"Someone show us all how to make a photocopy. Here," he said. A nickel was squeezed between his fingers. Sherry Warner raised her hand. She took the nickel from Professor Paine, dropped it into the copy machine, and stopped.

"What should I copy?" she asked.

"Anything," Professor Paine answered.

Sherry looked troubled.

"Here," Professor Paine said, pulling his billfold from his back pocket. He opened it and handed her a twenty-dollar bill. "Copy this."

"Money?" she said. "That's illegal."

"Take a walk on the wild side," Professor Paine said.

Sherry froze.

"Just stick it on there and push the damn button," Matt Gombie yelled. "The man wants to go fishing."

Professor Paine stood up and looked at Matt. "What's your name, young man?"

"Me?" Matt said. "Matt Gombie."

"Mr. Gombie," the professor said, nodding. "Are you by any chance a trout fisherman?"

Matt Gombie shook his head no. The professor shrugged and sat back down. "Go ahead," he said to Sherry, "copy away."

Sherry Warner pushed the button. The machine hummed, the light flashed, and a piece of white paper kicked out, a dark copy of the twenty-dollar bill in the middle.

"Very good," Professor Paine said.

"My name's Sherry Warner."

"Very good, Ms. Warner," the professor said, taking the photocopy from her hand. "Counterfeiting is a crime. You could be charged with a felony. How does that feel?"

"You *told* me to do it!"

The class laughed.

Professor Paine smiled at her. "How about the ditto machine, now? Can you finish the job?"

"What do you mean?"

"Here," he said, holding the photocopy out to her. "Make us two copies, or so. Double or triple our money."

Sherry refused, so Professor Paine selected another woman sitting in the front row, a pretty, recently divorced, older woman named Angela Childs. She looked to be about forty years old. On the nights she couldn't get a babysitter, she brought her two daughters, ages eight and ten, to class with her.

Angela made a tissue paper master on the Thermo Fax transparency machine, then hooked it to the ditto machine and quickly ran off four or five purple copies of the twenty-dollar bill. When she finished, she sat back down in her desk.

"Well, there we go," said Professor Paine. "The photocopier and the ditto machine. The best friends of teachers and the poor. I guess we're done. Any questions?"

Sherry Warner raised her hand. "Professor Paine," she said, "we're paying for this class and I, for one, resent being short-changed like this."

"Short-changed?" he said. "Whatever do you mean? We made a hundred dollars here tonight!"

We all laughed, but Sherry ignored him.

"Your infantile jokes and your lack of effort are really unprofessional," Sherry said.

"I take it you're the student who called Dean Gladdens last week to complain about my teaching."

Sherry said, "You gave me no choice."

"Well," Professor Paine said, "your passion for learning is commendable. Misguided, but commendable."

Matt Gombie raised his hand. "Professor Paine," Matt said, "just so you know, the brevity thing, it's cool. Don't think Miss Manners here is expressing majority opinion."

"Well, now," the professor said, "she does have a point, though, doesn't she? It is true that I will be retiring in the next few years. But, of course, I could put forth a little effort."

"Not necessary," Matt said. "Really. Things are cool the way they are."

"How about a bit of a lecture," Professor Paine said, "for old times' sake? Nothing too elaborate. Then next week I promise I'll have put together something worthwhile for the remaining four weeks or so of this summer term. We might as well learn something useful as long as we're all together, right? Ms. Warner, does that sound satisfactory?"

Sherry nodded. Matt exhaled loudly and slouched in his desk. Professor Paine stood and walked to a spot behind the lectern.

"You're all studying to be teachers," he began. "Few things in life are more gratifying or pleasurable than teaching." He paused. "Well, hell, let's be honest. Sex is a lot better, at least when you're young. Even with my ex-wives, on the rare occasions it happened, it wasn't too bad. Then, of course, there's trout fishing, which is far better still. Let's just agree to forget the gratifying and pleasurable part, and cut right to the chase.

"The thing about teaching that nobody tells you is that people don't like teachers. When you become a teacher, everyone with so-called normal jobs is going to envy you because you can spend all summer fishing. And they're going to resent even the little bit of money you make because it's what keeps their property taxes so high. Conservative newspaper columnists are going to write every week that public school education in America is a failure, forgetting to mention along the way that the people who taught them to write were public school teachers. They're going to refer to the teachers' union with the same sneer they use when talking about communists. In a nutshell, then, people are going to want you to teach their children everything they need to know to succeed, they're going to criticize how you do it, and they're going to try to pay you as little as possible for doing it. But that's America. Get used to it."

He paused to smile. "Any questions so far?" No one said anything. We all looked around the room at one another, as if deciding whether we should take notes or not.

"Now, my life, as you might have guessed by now, is in the toilet. Just as many of yours will be, someday. There's no avoiding it, really. It's the odds. Some lives are destined for happiness, and some lives end up in the toilet. Mine's one of the latter. I don't know how it happened.

One day I woke up to discover I'd gone from being a boy to being a man, and frankly, I liked being a boy better. It was a more soulful time. Less bullshit to wade through. The best thing manhood's got going for it is mortality. When you're young, you can't even imagine dying, but when you're older, unless you're balls deep in a river in the middle of a hatch, the idea doesn't seem so bad."

Sherry Warner raised her hand.

"Professor Paine," she said, "this has nothing to do with what you're supposed to be teaching us."

"On the contrary, Ms. Warner," he said, "this has everything to do with it. In fact, this will be the subject of class for the rest of the semester: Life. And to make it interesting, I'll tell you what. If you don't like what you learn, I'll give you your money back. What did you all pay, one hundred and twelve dollars per credit for this course, to learn what any eleven-year-old could teach you in an hour or two? How to use chalkboards and photocopy machines and VCRs? Shame on you!"

He was shouting and wandering back and forth like a crazy man. His tie flopped around against his chest like a fish, which, of course, is what it was.

"Teaching is not about how to write on the chalkboard or how to show a movie on the VCR!" he said. "Teaching is about passion! It is about pouring water on the human soul and watching it bloom! Your job as a teacher is not to make fancy bulletin boards or to write without squeaking the goddamn chalk but to liberate! To help your students build a self worthy of its humanity! Give them a fish and they'll have a fish fry; teach them to fish, and goddamnit, they'll have something to live for!"

Matt Gombie leaned over to me and whispered, "I don't understand this shit, do you?"

"It's better than learning how to lick chalk," I said.

"Dude," Matt said. "Good point." In truth, I found in Professor Paine a kindred soul. My life was spiraling down the toilet, too.

"Well," Professor Paine said, pausing to catch his breath. "There you have it. We'll start next week. I want everyone to come to class with a swimsuit and a towel. We'll meet at six o'clock in the Aquatic Center."

"At the pool?" Angela said. "What for?"

Professor Paine smiled. "To learn about life," he said. "We'll start with insects."

✖   ✖   ✖   ✖   ✖

One rarely sees college professors outside of the classroom, and then never when they're nearly naked. (Granted, some professors are occasionally seen naked by students, but they tend not to remain professors very long.) Professor Paine's skin looked like that of a raw chicken drumstick except for his neck and his arms, which were suntanned. A thick, pinkish scar ran down the center of his chest, and it looked like a nightcrawler stretched from his throat to six inches or so beneath his sternum.

"Quadruple bypass," he said, when he noticed me staring. "A souvenir from my third marriage." He held a one-gallon plastic ice cream bucket in his hands, with holes punched in the lid, and he wore baggy blue swimming trunks that made his legs look like sticks. Behind him was a plastic basket with scuba masks piled inside of it. "Gather over here, please," he said, as students in swimming suits wandered in. Only about twelve of us showed up, the others apparently deciding to drop the course and take it another time, when someone sane was teaching it. Four of the remaining students were women, including Sherry Warner, who wore a green, one-piece swimsuit, and rubber flip flops on her feet. She had her brown hair pinned up off of her neck, and she wore mother-of-pearl toenail polish. She gave me urges. I was glad the water in the pool was cold.

"Thank you all for coming," he said. "In the next four weeks, I'm going to do two things. I'm going to teach you how to teach. And I'm going to teach you how to fly-fish for trout. Both of these skills will be indispensable in your search to live a full and satisfying life."

We all nodded and looked around at one another. No one objected, not even Sherry Warner. We all stood in the chlorinated air in our swimsuits, arms crossed over our chests. The water in the pool was still and clear.

"Let's get in carefully on the shallow end." We did as we were told, one after another jumping in and standing in waist-deep water, with Professor Paine in front of us. He held his plastic bucket under one arm, with the basket of scuba masks partly submerged in the water in front of him. "Now, 90 percent of the food trout eat lives under water. The remaining 10 percent of the time, they feed on the surface. Dry fly-fishing targets that 10 percent. I'm going to teach you to become dry fly-fishermen and -women. It's as sublime an act as the creation of the world."

He held his plastic bucket in front of him. "To fish soulfully," he said, "you must first become entomologists. You must be able to identify and match, by size and color, thousands of insects. I will teach you the first six. Learning the rest—along with the nymphs, wet flies, streamers, and terrestrials trout will sometimes eat—will take the remainder of your life, but it will be worth it. Far better than sitting in a Laz-E-Boy in front of the tube, waiting to die." He pulled the cover from the bucket and tapped it, and hundreds of insects with clear, papery wings flew out and swirled around our heads. A few headed for the lights on the ceiling. The others stayed near the water. One landed on my lower lip and hung there, like a scar. Two of the women and one of the men—Matt Gombie—started waving their arms around their heads and hurried for the ladder to leave the pool.

"This is bullshit, man," Matt said, as he pulled himself from the water. "Bugs! I hate bugs!" He stood on the side of the pool and pointed to Professor Paine, who looked at him calmly. "You're nuts, man!" Matt yelled. "Deranged. Wacko. I can't believe they let you teach here!"

When this disturbance ended, we watched quietly as the insects Professor Paine had released—mayflies, caddis flies, mosquitoes, and assorted others—hovered over the surface of the pool. Sometimes they would settle delicately on the water, then fly up and hover for awhile before landing again. Professor Paine handed each of us a scuba mask, and put one on himself.

"Now, the thing to remember is that we don't see what trout see. To tie flies that accurately match living organisms, we must get beneath the surface to see and think like a trout. That is the secret to many things—we must seek to see the world from angles previously unattempted. On an actual river, most of these flies would be rising from the stream bottom, shedding the husks that covered them in the nymphal stage, and taking flight when they reached the surface. That is what we call a 'hatch.' Most live as flies for maybe three days, tops. In the air, they mate and the female lays eggs, which land in the water and sink to the bottom, starting the whole process over again. Once they mate, they die, and drop to the water. All of this sends trout into a feeding frenzy that is a wonder to behold. The only difference between mayflies and human beings, as far as I'm concerned, is that most of us never get into the air at all." He motioned to us. "Put on your masks and take a look. Make sure you hold your breath."

To tell the truth, I spent more time looking at Sherry Warner underwater than I did looking at mayflies. Her wet swimsuit clung to her body in a most generous manner, and tiny silver bubbles collected in the tiny hairs on her arms and legs. You couldn't see much of Professor

Paine's mayflies; just their legs and parts of their abdomens actually touched the water. The remaining parts of their bodies, and their wings, glimmered just above the surface, like a reflection on a pane of glass. Beneath the water, there was a clean line to everything, a softness and a slowness that relaxed me, a sense of perfect quiet.

We swam around for about forty-five minutes this way, sometimes pausing above the surface to catch our breath and to listen to Professor Paine lecture. He talked about light refraction and sight cones and line drag, and occasionally he discussed, with great reverence, insect hatches he'd witnessed on rivers named the Au Sable, the Beaverkill, the Blackfoot, and the Bow. Eventually, two more students got out of the pool and headed home. Professor Paine ignored them.

When we had showered and dressed again, Professor Paine led us to our classroom, where we sat in our desks as he distributed small fly-tying kits to each of us—there were just seven students left, four women and three men, our wet hair still smelling of chlorine, our faces still marked by red lines where the scuba masks had pressed against the skin. Inside these fly-tying kits were assorted spools of thread, a bobbin, tweezers, tiny fishing hooks, small cellophane bags of fur and feathers, scissors, and tiny tubes of head cement. A small vise was also included, along with a magnifying glass mounted on a pivoting rod, which could be lowered over the tip of the vise, where the hook would be secured. I could see my fingerprints through this magnifying glass, unexplored territory, little whorls of ridges like the elevation markings on a topographic map. Professor Paine passed out photocopied instructions and photographs which explained how to tie six dry flies: an Adams; a March Brown; a Hexagenia mayfly; an Elk Hair Caddis; a Royal Coachman; and a Trico.

Professor Paine took us through the process of tying an Elk Hair Caddis that first night. "An elk's hair is hollow," he said, "and filled with air. It's as if God intended it should be used to make dry flies, which must float. But really, you can tie flies with anything. There's a German Shepard in my neighborhood that wanders loose, and sometimes I coax him close and buzz a bit of hair from his back—great stuff for wet flies. My ex-wife has a tortoise-shell cat with hair like marabou—Checkers, she calls him. I tie a great leech with that stuff, a Checkers Leech, I call it. My ex thinks her cat loses patches of hair because it has problems with stress."

The first time through, Sherry tied the most impressive Elk Hair Caddis, each hair in place. Mine looked like a glob of goo left over after a cat eats a mouse. I could not get the hair to stand properly. When Professor Paine saw it, he smiled and shook his head. "Try again," he said to me. "And don't get discouraged. We're imitating God's perfection here. It's good to be humbled; it makes the world a grander place."

It took me four more attempts to tie a fly that looked remotely like the picture on the instructions. Our homework was to tie the remaining five flies before class the following week. Professor Paine wrote his telephone number and address on the chalkboard, and told us to feel free to call him for help if we needed it. He also encouraged us to trade telephone numbers, and urged us to contact one another for help. I traded numbers with Sherry Warner. I called her four times. The fifth time, she said, "Why don't you just come to my room and I'll show you."

I went. Her fingers were long and slender. Her hair smelled like apricots. She sat cross-legged in a chair at her desk in blue jeans and a t-shirt, and I stood behind her, watching, breathing her in. The flies she tied were lovely. She tied two extra Hexagenias, cut the barbs off of the hooks, and pushed them through her pierced ears to wear as earrings.

In the classroom the next week, Professor Paine inspected the flies of the three students who remained in the class, Sherry Warner, myself, and Angela Childs. He did not seem at all bothered by the high student attrition rate, and commented nonchalantly that eleven students had requested their money back and that he'd paid them, as promised.

Sherry's flies were beautiful. Even the twin hairs that protruded from the tail of her Trico—a tiny thing about the size of a fruit fly—were tied exactly as they should have been. Professor Paine complimented the work that Angela and I did as well, but it was obvious we had more work to do.

In the remaining time that class period, which lasted to nearly midnight, Professor Paine introduced us to all of the equipment a fly-fisherman or -woman would need on the river. He showed us all of his own equipment—his neoprene waders, his Orvis graphite flyrod, his fishing vest, filled with fly boxes and other necessities, his split willow creel, his cherry-handled landing net. He taught us to tie knots in tippet material as fine as Sherry Warner's hair. He also showed us home videos he took of his son pulling in beautiful brook trout in the early morning on a small, meadow stream, and large, angry-looking brown trout caught at night on the White River. As I watched, sitting there in the dark, I felt as I did as a boy, on Saturday mornings in springtime after my father left for work, when the newly-green world waited for me to dirty my knees in its glorious mud.

We met once more at the Aquatic Center in our swimsuits, where Professor Paine taught us fly-casting. Each of us received an hour-long lesson while the other two watched from the side of the pool and answered questions.

"The rhythm of proper flycasting is like the rhythm of a heartbeat at rest," Dr. Paine said. "If you are in love, so much the better. Your heart will beat more strongly, and your casting will reflect your love. Your right arm and wrist are the metronome, but your heart sets the tempo." He demonstrated as he spoke. "You lift the line from the water, move the rod backward to one o'clock, wait for the line to load, then move forward to eleven o'clock again, and release." He did. The line floated in a perfect, tight loop, uncoiling to set the fly softly on the surface of the pool, between the diving boards.

Angela went first, and Professor Paine stood closely on her left side, reaching around her, guiding her right arm with his hand on her elbow. She laughed as he did when she began her forward cast too quickly, snapping the line behind her like a bullwhip. But after a half-hour or so, he was standing six feet away from her, and Angela was casting confidently. All this time, I sat next to Sherry Warner at poolside, my left knee just brushing against her leg.

"Sherry and William!" Professor Paine would shout to us, occasionally. "Tell me the proper size variations of an Elk-Hair Caddis."

"Size twelve to size eighteen," we said, in unison, "with size sixteen preferred."

"Very good. What about a Trico?"

"Size twenty to twenty-four."

"Excellent. And what is the latin name for the Hex mayfly?"

"*Hexagenia limbata*," we answered.

"Nicely done!" Professor Paine said. "And what is the preferred casting motion to prevent over-casting?"

"From eleven o'clock to one o'clock," Sherry said.

"Good," Professor Paine said. "Come in here and show me. William, you may come in as well. You can see better from in here." I could not tell if he meant I could better see Sherry Warner or her casting motion. Perhaps both. Then he smiled at Angela. "You cast wonderfully, dear," he said to her. "There are few things so lovely or graceful as a beautiful woman with an expensive fly rod in her hand, using it well."

At the end of class that evening, nearly midnight, Professor Paine announced that our final exams would be held the following weekend, if that was possible for everyone. We would meet at his house on Friday morning, ride together to Gander Mountain to purchase the necessary equipment, then head north some three hundred miles to the Brule River in northern Wisconsin for two days to fish for trout. The Brule River, he said, was worthy water, the kind of stream John might have chosen in which to baptize Jesus, (assuming, of course, a hatch was not taking place, in which case the baptism would have had to wait awhile). Bald eagles soared over the Brule, he said, and the flesh of brook trout pulled from its waters was as orange as fresh tangerines.

I had to borrow money from my father to purchase my fishing equipment. I told him my "Instructional Technologies" class had turned out to be incredibly interesting, and that I needed money for class supplies. He readily passed along his Mastercard, pleased I had discovered a passion for my education major after all.

That weekend, the four of us drove north in Professor Paine's Ford Explorer, and we camped along the Brule River in a large dome tent set up on a bed of soft, rust-colored pine needles. The air smelled like cedar and fresh water, and the river was the most beautiful thing I'd ever seen. Professor Paine spent most of his time with Angela, which was fine with Sherry Warner and me. We went off by ourselves upstream, through several slow, languorous pools, and downstream of a small rapids we found some brook trout that rose to our Elk Hair Caddis flies as fast as we tossed them. Sherry taught me to set the hook by raising my rod quickly, but gently, on the rise.

Sherry Warner and I spent a lot of time together that weekend. We caught fish, cleaned them, and ate them fried in butter over an open fire. That first evening, to our great fortune, we witnessed a brief hatch of Hexagenia mayflies—*Hexagenia limbata*—huge, thick-bodied mayflies that fluttered in our flashlight beams like bats. We stood in the flowing river in the dark, tossing our Hex patterns wherever we heard brown trout slurping or splashing on the surface, and Sherry and I each caught and released about a half-dozen browns, the largest over twenty inches. Professor Paine and Angela sat on a rock on the shoreline holding citronella candles, laughing and clapping each time we hooked a fish and each time we missed one. He and Angela went back to the tent early, and Sherry Warner and I kept casting under the moon, pausing, sometimes, just to listen to the sound of everything.

I got an A in "Instructional Technologies" that semester. So did Angela Childs and Sherry Warner. But the story doesn't end there. Just as the fall semester was about to begin—I had switched majors again, and for awhile had hopes of becoming an ichthyologist— I learned that Professor Paine had been excused from his teaching post. Near the end of the summer, Matt Gombie had filed a grievance against him for unprofessional conduct, and the university administration, moved to action after learning that Angela Childs had moved in with him, found him guilty and initiated expulsion hearings. Dean Gladdens testified that Professor Paine sometimes spent only fifteen minutes of a three-hour course actually teaching it. Someone else reported that he'd once allowed his eleven-year-old son to substitute teach for him, and that he sometimes got his kicks by secretly shaving patches of body hair from dogs and cats. To avoid expulsion, and the loss of benefits that would bring, Professor Paine took an early retirement and moved with Angela, her children, and his son, to Helena, Montana, to be near the finest inland trout waters in North America. I never heard from him again.

A year later, Sherry Warner and I got married. Some people are surprised when they hear that part of the story. And most people believe that our story must end like a TV movie-of-the-week: that inspired by Professor Paine, Sherry and I must have gone on to become award-winning teachers, who show our students how to look beneath the surface of things. I always nod at that point and tell them they're half right, that Sherry is a gifted high school teacher. More importantly, I tell them, she can tie dry flies that look so alive they seem to move and breathe as they dance over rushing freestone rivers and float down tranquil, meadow streams. She is an artist with feathers and hair and thread, and I show her work whenever I can at the finest river-galleries in the world, populated by the most discriminating of buyers.

And me, well, I never did become a teacher. I never even graduated from college. But thanks to Professor Paine, I found my calling.

I became a trout fisherman.

H

unger at the End of Life

It was not enough that he should endure his wife's slow death, but this now, too—this mysterious visitation, a frenzied rustling above the ceiling each evening at nightfall. Ralph could only guess what it might be: mice, chipmunks, squirrels. Could be anything. Years ago, a neighbor's attic had been overrun by opossums. The previous morning, Ralph had stood outside and gazed up at the eaves of his house, found the hole where a large knot had been knocked free of the cedar soffit, room enough for any number of small creatures to pass through, certainly. But what? And how many?

He had no time for this.

For the past six days, his wife Clara—who, at sixty-eight, was five years younger than Ralph—lay dying in a rented hospital bed in their dining room beneath a clear, steady drip of morphine. The hospice workers who arrived each morning with their thermoses of coffee assured him he was doing the right thing. No, they shook their heads, reassuringly, he was not starving her to death. Of course not. Ralph had read somewhere that starving to death was among the most painful ways to die. The body slowly consumed its own muscle tissue with an excruciating, internal flame. The doctor, too, had assured him that withholding nourishment in cases like these was the most loving, humane course of action. Clara's body would live on five or six days, perhaps a day or two longer. If it were my wife, the doctor had said, one hand on Ralph's quaking shoulder, I'd do the same.

But what they didn't know was how he and Clara had once eaten together! In Paris, in New Orleans, in Chicago—such food they had shared! And far before then, when they were young and too poor to travel, the way their hungry mouths had feasted on one another, how they had kissed with lips bloodied by the force of desire after absences as short as a day at work, a physical love that had burned for decades. How often had he drunk from the warm spring between her legs, water that glowed with the scent of baking bread, her velvety flesh soft against his mouth, flesh which had brought forth no children for all their trying, but no matter, now. And how many nights, afternoons, mornings, had Clara taken him into her mouth playfully, lovingly, had said, "Don't be so damned shy." Had said, "Don't hold back, Rafer. Please don't." And he watched as she drew him in, made him open up to her, leave his own skin, watched until he melted in her mouth, salty and opalescent. Like the flesh of oysters, Clara said. My God, Ralph thought. *My God.*

She had fed him through forty-two years of marriage, baked dozens of birthday cakes, hundreds of pies, thousands of cookies, casseroles, muffins, flipped a room full of pancakes, golden and steaming in the skillet. Each spring, Clara had gathered mounds of asparagus that grew wild in the country ditches, steamed the spears a vibrant green and served them slathered in melted butter. Each fall, she'd pick the shiny, red hips of wild roses, ground and steeped them in tea which she sipped all winter, sometimes while reading novels aloud to him in bed.

So now each evening at suppertime Ralph sat at Clara's bedside, and instead of eating, he told her stories of their finest meals together.

Perhaps he got some of the details wrong—she would have quickly corrected any mistakes, he thought, smiling—but like so much that is genuine, joyful memories were enhanced by their imperfections. He began with the story of their first meal together in France. At Alcazar, a former Paris cabaret in the sixth arrondissement, on the rue Mazarine, they had eaten green beans in a lemony vinaigrette, duckling medallions in cognac cream sauce, and melting chocolate cake with lavender ice cream. He spoke of fenneled sea bass and prawns in New Orleans; crabs pulled from the Wye River in Maryland, their slate blue shells laid open with little wooden hammers as Ralph and Clara sat overlooking the harbor in Baltimore.

"Remember our last dinner in Paris?" he asked, Clara's sixth evening home, his chin resting against her arm. He smoothed the gray hair from her temple, brushed it back off her face. "Do you remember it Clara, my love?" he whispered, his lips brushing her ear. "Last summer, our final night, we went to Les Olivades, on avenue Segur, in the seventh. I was tired but you'd insisted we go. We didn't even arrive until after ten because we'd been to a concert in Ste.Chapelle—Vivaldi played so beautifully it made you cry." He smiled at the memory. "The lettuce salad came with salmon and crawfish, sliced pears and shaved Granny Smith apples. I had roasted quail in a fig and red wine sauce. Your main course was pasta with fire-roasted vegetables. What enchantment as we walked out at midnight, our legs wobbly, our brains warmed by the wine, to find the Eiffel Tower lit up and shining! Remember that, my sweet girl?"

Ralph looked into her passive face. Even in sleep, her consciousness deft and alive with dreams, Clara's beauty had entranced him. But this was something less than sleep. Her beauty seemed now the flat, silent beauty of a photograph. Ralph shook his head and smiled. "Such a delicious life we've had, Clara," he said. "Eating together, talking of books, music, sex—all the necessities, as you called them."

The sun had dropped and above him, once again, he heard the muffled scratching and clawing in the attic. In the darkness of rafters and insulation, something came alive. Ralph listened for awhile, annoyed that Clara's final days and hours should be so disturbed. Then he kissed his wife on the lips, settled into the twin bed he had set up beside hers, and closed his eyes.

In the morning, Clara's seventh at home, Ralph awoke early, the world's light still gray, and was startled by some small, shadowed movement over his wife. He sat up, blinked back the haze of sleep in his eyes.

Something small and dark seemed to emerge from the center of Clara's chest. He reached beneath the bed, struggled to locate his glasses. What was this? Was he dreaming? He imagined Clara's spirit rising from her body. Perhaps, even, her soul. His hand found the metal frame of his glasses. He put them on.

A small, brown bat clung to the white linens covering Clara's chest, its wings held in an arch over its head, like a broken, black umbrella. The bat stood little higher than a large coffee mug, but it frightened Ralph. He hissed at it as he struggled to his feet, swinging stiffly with one hand, and the bat flashed into the air and left the dining room. It circled the kitchen ceiling, then entered the living room and disappeared, perching inside a lampshade.

Ralph sat down on his bed and blinked. Bats, he thought. Not squirrels or mice. Of course.

He stood again, his back and neck stiff, his muscles weak, kissed Clara on the forehead, then ambled gingerly into the living room. He opened the windows and removed the screens, letting them fall outside behind the bushes. A light dusting of frost coated the grass. He opened the windows in the bedrooms, then did the same in the kitchen, in the library. Cool, late September air flowed into the house. He put on his robe, found a flyswatter in the pantry.

Ralph returned to the living room, crouched, moved slowly, stalking the lampshade. As he dropped to one knee to peer beneath it, the bat exploded out the top and quickly flew toward the ceiling. Ralph swung at it awkwardly. Clean miss. But after circling the room twice, the bat dropped down and flew out through an open window.

Ralph closed the window behind it, leaving the screens for later, then closed the other windows in the house. Cold air had already reached the thermostat. In the basement, he could hear the furnace come to life, the flames roaring inside their steel box, the fan pushing warm air through the ticking ductwork.

"We've got bats in our belfry, darling," he said aloud. From the distance, he could see her catheter sack hooked to the frame of the bed, its meager contents the color of rust. He looked at the mantle clock. Six-thirty. The hospice people would arrive in thirty minutes. Ralph dressed, then sat beside Clara's bed and told her the story of a breakfast they'd once eaten in St. Paul, one of her favorites, fresh cranberry muffins and a fruit salad of blueberries, mangoes, and coconut milk. After he'd finished, he formulated a plan—a half-baked plan, Clara would have called it—to rid the house of bats. Ralph smiled, remembering how Clara often teased him for the clumsy way he attended to what she called men's work, anything that required high climbing, heavy lifting, or a motor.

When the hospice team arrived, Ralph greeted them at the door, then left the house. In the garage, he set up his stepladder beneath the trap door that led into the attic. He found his Sears Shop Vac, a thirty-gallon model he'd used for years to clean up sawdust and dirt from the garage. He removed the cover, emptied its contents into the trash, then plugged it in, running a fifty-foot extension cord from the outlet to the vacuum. He climbed the ladder empty-handed, struggled to remove the trap door, his arms quivering with the weight, then came back down to retrieve the vacuum. With the hose of the Shop Vac wrapped loosely around his neck and the drum dangling from one arm, he began his struggle up the ladder.

The effort exhausted him, and he knew why: He had not eaten for six days, would not—could not—eat while denying Clara nourishment, though he had continued to drink a glass of water every few hours. The cramps and pangs of hunger had been agonizing, but even worse was the weakness had settled into his body. The empty vacuum couldn't weigh more than five or ten pounds, but he could barely keep his grip on it.

Sweat trickled down his face as he climbed into the attic, lunging with a final burst of energy to pull the canister in after him. He sat dripping, his breath heaving, his heart pounding rapidly, waiting for his eyes to adjust to the darkness. Gradually, he was able to see. Rafters, smooth and evenly spaced as ribs, stretched into darkness. And there they were: bats, dozens of them, hanging upside down along the rafters like little, black sausages wrapped in waxed paper. Ralph stood up, hunched over, walked slowly along the floor joists and insulation to where they rested. The bats shifted nervously as he approached, but did not fly. Slowly, he raised the mouth of the vacuum over his shoulders, pointed it at the nearest bats, and flipped the switch.

The vacuum roared and the bats exploded into flight in all directions. He ducked instinctively, crouched and waved the vacuum nozzle blindly overhead as they flew in a blizzard all about him. He realized, quickly, the futility of his efforts, and he smiled to himself, thinking of how Clara would have laughed and laughed. What had he been thinking? What a ridiculous idea. He turned off the vacuum, waited ten or fifteen minutes while the bats settled in again. Ralph struggled back down the ladder and sat on the garage floor until he had strength enough to return to the house for a shower.

That afternoon, Clara began to die. Her breathing grew irregular, became a struggle. Her eyes never opened. Over several hours, life simply left her, in the slow, gradual way afternoon merges into evening. Ralph held her hand, spoke to her tenderly, and then she was gone. In minutes her small, dry hand began to cool under his, as if the soul itself were the source of the body's fire. He sat with her, crying, until twilight, then called the funeral home. He watched as they carried her body into the waiting car and drove her away.

As the sun fell, Ralph put on a coat and walked outside, sat down in the cool grass of the back yard. He'd stopped crying, though he felt as if he might start again at any time. The warm smoke of his breath dissolved in the air, and he sat watching the hole in the eaves of his house, waiting for nightfall.

Crickets and other insects began to sing. The woods hummed with the whine of mosquitoes. And then as he watched, the bats began to appear, plunging out of the hole one by one by one, like paratroopers, their wings churning air as they darted out over the fields. He counted sixty-two bats in all, amazed, enthralled by their numbers, by their erratic, frenetic flight.

When fifteen minutes passed and no more bats had emerged, Ralph rose and walked into the garage to retrieve his ladder. He propped it against the house, climbed carefully, holding a small, pine board under his arm, his hammer in one hand, four nails clutched between his teeth. He covered the hole with the wood and nailed it in place. He descended the ladder, carried it back into the garage.

Alone inside his silent house, he removed his coat, turned on the kitchen light, and went to the stove. Ralph lit the front burner with a wooden match the way Clara had done thousands of times, the blue flames blooming from the center like the vibrant petals of an aster. He found a can of soup in the pantry, sat at the kitchen table, worked the opener around the lid by hand. His stomach churned, an ache that felt something like love.

Ralph poured the soup into a shallow saucepan, set it over the fire, and waited for the broth to boil. He held a spoon in his hand as he waited, his returning hunger, modest though it was, Clara's parting gift to him.

Like Water
Becoming Air

The ad in *The Birmingham News* says "VAN FOR SALE, Dodge *Caravan*, 1998, forty-seven thousand miles, blue, air, am fm, cd, like new. $2,000." Just two grand! Damn. Must be a misprint. I take a pull off my joint and dial the number. A man answers and says that's right, son, two thousand dollars. I hang up and drive out there, a sound like bees buzzing softly inside my temples.

It's raining hard, those big, gelatin drops splattering on the windshield, and the wipers on my *Nova* don't work. The rubber's all screwed up, so it's like I'm driving through a waterfall the whole way. But soon enough I'm in Mountain Brook, surrounded by big brick houses set back in the woods, curvy concrete driveways, swimming pools, statues of little jockeys holding lanterns. When my mom wasn't drinking, she used to clean houses for people like this. Now she can't even keep her own house clean. Not that I care.

The guy meets me at the door, gives me the keys, says take it for a spin, son. So I take it downtown to Gorilla—that's Randy, he's huge and hairy, and can fit a whole cheeseburger in his mouth, which makes him The Man in the crowd I run with. Works at Larry's Mobil on Southside. He just pumps gas, but sometimes they let him do an oil change if things get busy. He thinks this makes him a mechanic.

We want A VAN dinkwad, he says, at first. You know, a Chevy van, has shag carpet inside, skulls and guitars and shit painted on the outside. A van-van, not one of these yuppie egg cartons.

But it's just two grand, I tell him. The magic words. He can't believe it. So he goes into the office to check the blue book. A lady pulls up while he's on the phone, so I get stuck filling her Lincoln *Town Car* with unleaded premium. She makes me check her oil, the tires, her wiper fluid. Cold rain pounding my back the whole time. Randy comes out when I'm done.

Blue book's almost nine grand on this sonofabitch, he says. Must be something wrong with it. Must have a cracked frame, or something.

Randy drops to one knee and his head disappears underneath the van. He gets up, pops the hood, and looks at the engine.

Shit, he says. Looks almost new. Maybe it's hot.

No way, I tell him. The guy's rich. You should have seen the place.

He looks at me and raises his eyebrows.

So what should we do? I ask. Randy's more or less the leader. Me, Dave, and Piranha—his real name's Peter but he chomped some guy's finger in a fight, teeth sunk right to the bone, so we call him Piranha—we usually do what Randy says. This bothers me sometimes, but it's not like I can do much about it.

Let's buy it, Gorilla says. Even if there is something wrong, it's worth a hell of a lot more than two grand.

Driving back into Mountain Brook, I've got Springsteen cranked so loud on the radio I can feel the bass drum on my skin. It's still raining hard and I'm shivering—my clothes are actually steaming—but when I knock on the door, the guy doesn't invite me in, doesn't want me dripping on his clean floors. He makes me feel stupid at first, because he just stares at me like he can't quite remember me and knows he should. He looks at me hard. Could be because my long hair looks like a bowl of wet spaghetti someone just dumped on my head. It's blonde, white almost. Some people call me Al-bino, because I don't go out in the sun. My skin stays so white people say it looks transparent, like plastic wrap.

Behind this guy, who looks rich with his graying hair and tweedy sports jacket and even smells rich, like expensive aftershave, I see his wife walk up. She looks as if she just got out of bed. She's wearing a long, pink, silky robe that drags on the floor, her hair's all messed up, and she's got puffy shadows like two little mice are asleep under her eyes. She says something, but he ignores her. I can't hear what she says because the rain's hissing all around me.

Will you take an offer? I yell at him.

Price is firm son, he says. We're giving it away as it is.

He wants it off his driveway. That driveway's cleaner than the floor in my mother's kitchen.

Two grand, then.

Sold, he says. Sold. Just like that. He shakes my hand. I offer him twenty bucks for a security deposit, but he pushes it away and says, I trust you, son. I tell him I'll be back with the money the next afternoon.

And then something weird happens. There's a loud noise behind him, and his wife rushes past him, pushes him out the door, and grabs me by the shoulders. Before I can do anything she hugs me hard right there on their porch, with the rain splattering both of us. Fisher! she says. She locks her arms around my neck and squeezes, her hair covering my face. I stagger backward and almost fall down.

Her husband shouts something and appears at my side. He's tugging harshly on her hands, trying to pry her off of me. She's holding on hard, her arms like broomsticks cutting into the back of my neck.

For God's sake, he says, yelling at her. Let go! For God's sake!

He finally pulls her free, spins her toward the house, forces her back inside. He's got her elbows pinned at her sides. She wails something but in the din of the rain I can't understand what she's saying. She's yelling like a crazy woman.

He leans forward and closes the door behind him, holds onto the knob so it can't be turned from the inside. I'm sorry, he says. His hair is messed up. He looks like he might cry.

I nod, rubbing the back of my neck with one hand. What the hell was that all about? I ask.

He pauses for a moment, looks over his shoulder at the door. She's not feeling well, he says. I'm sorry about that. I'll have the title and owner's manual ready for you tomorrow. Then he goes back inside and closes the door behind him.

That night, my friends and I get together at Dave's house to celebrate. His parents are off at his aunt's or something, so we crank the tunes and fire up the bong right at the kitchen table. It goes around, four, five, six times. My eyes start prickling, my ears get warm, and already, I'm in the comfort zone, feeling like a thousand spiders are stringing cobwebs in my brain.

Since high school, it was something we'd talked about. We'd get out, get jobs, and after we all got hot cars, we'd pool our money to buy a van and cruise around in it on the weekends, picking up babes and getting high. Of course, none of us has ever picked up a girl in his life. We're pathetic that way. I had a nice girlfriend once. Gloria. But it didn't last too long. She was one of those girls always on you to do something with your life. I want to be a writer and Gloria was always telling me I could be one, I just had to apply myself. You can be anything you want to be, she would say. Hold fast to dreams, she would say. Man. What is it with girls and that dreamy shit? Thinking about Gloria, though, still makes me feel like a swan is trying to open her wings and fly inside me, so I try not to think of her.

Goes to show you what a bunch of potheads can do when they put their minds to it, Piranha says.

Damn straight! Dave says, standing barefoot on his mother's kitchen table, playing air guitar. We're listening to Bachman Turner Overdrive, weird, retro stuff. My ma says it's what she and my dad, wherever he is, used to listen to in high school. Electric guitars buzzing like a million June bugs on a thousand screen doors.

Gorilla pours a bag of potato chips into the pouch he's made in the front of his greasy Mobil t-shirt, and starts eating chips by the handfuls. He takes a potato chip from his shirt and sets it on the table. This is your brain, he shouts, over the music. With the greasy palm of his hand he smashes that chip into powder. This is your brain on drugs, he says. He laughs and looks at me. I give him a half smile but don't say anything.

What's the matter, Hemingway? he says. He calls me that because he knows it bugs me. He makes fun of my wanting to be a writer.

Nothing's the matter, I say. But it's not true. Pot does this to me sometimes. I float outside of myself, like those people who supposedly have near-death experiences, and hover above the room. I hate what I see, but I can't seem to change the view. If my life came with a remote I'd have it in my hand all the time. A hundred fifty channels and nothing on.

I said what the hell's your problem? Gorilla shouts, tapping me on the shoulder.

No problem, I tell him.

Leave him alone, man, Piranha says to him. Randy shrugs and stuffs his mouth full of potato chips, then opens his mouth at me so

I can see the mess on his tongue.

But by the time I get back home, my mom is passed out in a dirty t-shirt and blue jeans on the sofa. Her hair, an inch of black roots and the rest blonde, is tangled over her face. I can't tell if her boyfriend's been over or not. Nothing but static on the TV screen. All the ashtrays full. Empty beer cans all over. I try to wake her, but it's useless. I brush the hair softly from her face and kiss her on the forehead. I wander into her bedroom, pull a blanket off her mattress, and cover her.

By the light of the fuzz on the TV, I empty the ashtrays into the kitchen trash can, then stack the empty beer cans on top of that. I turn off the TV and go to bed.

After work the next day—I bag groceries and stock shelves at Winn-Dixie—I hop in the *Nova* and drive over to Dave's to pick him up. He's going to drive my car back when I pick up the van. It's two o'clock, and my head's buzzing because I had to be in that morning at five to help unload the produce, and I only slept two or three hours. I had to drink a gallon of coffee and take some No-Doz to stay awake, but it didn't help much. I dropped some lady's canned ham on a dozen eggs—splat!—clear slime all over everything else in the bag. The cashier got in my face about it, and the customer threw a fit, too, like one bag of slimy groceries is going to ruin the world. And then at lunch, Mr. Penfield—the manager—tells me to get my hair cut, OR ELSE. It's about the tenth time he's threatened me this month. He means it this time, he says. Uh-huh.

When we leave Dave's I've got $2,000 cash in my pocket—five hundred apiece from the four of us—and we head out to Mountain Brook.

Nice fucking house, Dave says, when we get to the place. Dave drops me and takes off, because he's got to get back to town for the afternoon shift at the shoe store where he works. In good weather, this house looks even bigger than the last time I saw it. On the bottom, it's red and black brick. On top, white stucco and huge wooden beams. It looks like a ski lodge in Switzerland or something. Out back, an old Black guy shaped like a question mark is vacuuming the swimming pool. He's standing on the edge with a long, silver tube that sticks up out of the water, over his head, and he's pushing it and pulling it slowly across the bottom. He waves to me as I disappear behind the hedge. I knock on the front door.

The man I met before isn't home, but his wife lets me in. She's dressed nicely this time, your typical, middle-aged Mountain Brook lady, I guess. Lots of make-up, lipstick. She's got a flowery dress on, her silvery hair's pulled back into a bow, and her fingernails are perfect, and painted this peach color. She smells like that smell you get from the perfume ads when you open a women's magazine.

When I walk in the door, the first thing I see is a huge table in the front hallway. On top of the table is this pyramid of about fifty—fifty!—framed pictures of this blonde guy. Two lights in the ceiling above the table illuminate the photographs: Naked pictures of him as a little baby. Vacation pictures of him growing up in front of Mickey Mouse, Mount Rushmore, the Eiffel Tower, the Golden Gate Bridge, all kinds of places I've never been. Pictures of him in a tuxedo. In his high school football uniform. Waterskiing. With his arm around some hot babe in a bikini.

The woman pauses for awhile, to let me look, I guess, then leads me into the dining room, where the owner's manual, the title, and the maintenance records for the van are arranged on the table.

Sit down, please, she says. Is this everything you need?

Looks great, I tell her. I take the money out of my pocket and count it out on the table. Twenty bills. But when I try to hand her the cash, she starts crying. Sobbing. Her hands are folded on her lap, her body's shaking, and these clear trickles—they look like airplane glue—are making little tracks through the powder on her face. Her mascara starts to break away, little black icebergs that join the flow.

I'm sorry, she says. She wipes her tears with her fingertips, smearing mascara across her cheeks. Then she grabs my shoulder and squeezes. Makes me jump, really. You look just like my son! she says.

I know right away who she's talking about. The guy in the shrine by the front door. She's right, too. We do look alike, though he's a lot more clean cut than me. With my mop of hair and Megadeath t-shirt, I look like some reefer madness version of her kid, which maybe I am, at least on the outside.

May I get you some iced tea? she asks. She's staring at me hard. Gloria used to look at me that way. It makes me want to run. Before I can answer, though, she stands and walks to the kitchen. I've still got the money in my hand, and I put it on the table where she had been sitting. The money feels soft, like flannel.

In a minute she comes back with my tea. It's good and cold, in this tall, heavy, cut crystal glass with ice and a piece of lemon and some lemon seeds floating in it. It's the most beautiful glass I've ever had in my hand. The woman sits back down. She's stopped crying, at least for the moment, and she wipes her nose with a tissue.

You're really my son, she says. Aren't you?

I shake my head. No I'm not, I tell her.

Well then why would you just show up at my door? It doesn't make sense. You look just like him.

I look like a lot of people, I tell her. Some people think I look like Tom Petty. Or if I was a little heavier, I'd look like Greg Allman from the old Allman Brothers Band.

She nods. You look like Fisher, too, she says. My Fisher was a wonderful boy. Full of mischief. When he was eight he liked to ride his bicycle off of the diving board into the pool.

I think to myself, maybe I don't want to get into this conversation. I want to take the papers and get the heck out of here. I'd like to know what happened to this Fisher, actually, but this woman has me feeling weird.

She says, Be careful, I always used to say. Fisher, be careful. Fisher be careful. I sounded like a parrot. She laughs. One time, on my forty-sixth birthday, my husband surprised me with a new car, an Audi. While he and I were out to dinner, Fisher and his friends gift-wrapped it in aluminum foil. They used over one-hundred boxes! The car looked silver plated. When the sun came up, the car was so bright you couldn't even look at it without hurting your eyes. *The Birmingham News* came out and took pictures.

She stops talking for awhile, because she's crying again. I reach over and touch her elbow softly with my fingers.

Fisher! she says again, and lunges at me. She tries to hug me again, but I pull free. I grab the papers for the van and the keys, and I jump out of the chair and head for the door.

Wait! she says, and follows behind me. We can be friends!

Outside, the sunlight burns my eyes. But getting out of that house makes me feel like I can breathe again. The woman doesn't follow me outside. Instead, she stops at the door. It's like there's some force field there, holding her in. She stands waving at me, tears running down her face. It makes my stomach hurt.

I walk around the hedge and the pool man is standing on the drive-way with a garden hose, watering the azaleas. He's wearing sunglasses and a Braves baseball cap.

When he sees me, he turns off the hose and stares. He looks at one side of my face, then leans to see the other side. Goddamn! he says. You look just like. . . .

Yeah, I know, I tell him. My name's Al.

He laughs and puts one hand on his chest. You about gave me a heart attack, boy.

He pokes the hose at the keys in my hand. You bought the van, too, didn't you?

Yes I did.

That van belonged to him. Safest vehicle in America. Got that air bag in it, you know. Crash into something and it blows up right in front of you, like a feather pillow. Fisher didn't want it. He wanted something flashy—a *Trans Am*, a Corvette, you know, what I call dick-hard cars. Young men all the same, out to impress the ladies.

What happened to him? I ask.

Last September, he went to Atlanta with some girl to see a basketball game, and his daddy let him take the Mercedes, a convertible, to impress the girl. Driving home, Fish fell asleep and drove under the back end of a semi trailer stopped on the side of the highway. Cut his head clean off. If he'd been in this van, it wouldn't have happened. Been like a funeral around here ever since. Glad to see they're letting it go.

He points to the house. Like yesterday to her, though. She won't even come outside. Left the van sitting here, too, as if leaving it be would bring him back. He looks at me. Goddamn boy! You sure you ain't him, coming back here to scare my black ass off?

No, I'm not anyone. Just myself.

He smiles. Well all right, he says. If you say so.

I party with my friends in the van long into the night. We drive it all over town. We've all got keys, and we cut cards to see who gets to take it home the first night. Wavy Dave wins. I come in third. All night, though, I keep thinking about that woman, about that boy getting himself killed. I don't tell my friends about it, because it would make them laugh out loud, the thought of him losing his head that way, and I really couldn't handle that.

When I get home, at about three in the morning, I can hardly stand up, I'm so tired. My mother and her boyfriend are fighting in her bedroom. Things are hitting the walls. Lamps, shoes, the usual. I turn around to leave, think about sleeping in my car, which I've done before, but I'm exhausted. So I close the door, drop into bed. I take a few sleeping pills and a couple aspirin, but they don't seem to help. My ears are ringing, and the back of my head throbs. Eventually, Mom and Dick stop fighting, but I almost prefer the screaming to the sounds that come next. After they finish, I hear first my mother, then Dick walk into the bathroom, and I know what he has dangling from his fingers. The toilet flushes. Sometimes, Dick, who's a big, heavy guy with some major tattoos, forgets to flush, and in the morning I find his condom hanging in the water like the shed skin of a snake.

A knock at my door. Mom pokes her head in. Some woman called on the phone tonight, she says. Said she needs to see you.

Gloria? For a moment, I'm hopeful. I wipe my eyes with my fingers.

No. No, not Gloria. Her name was, oh, what the hell was it? Jane, I think. Jean, Jane, Joan. I can't remember her goddamn name. I told her she can find you at work tomorrow. My mom squints at me. What's wrong with you?

Nothing, I tell her.

You sure?

I nod. She shrugs and closes the door.

In the morning, I'm on my knees at the store putting thirty-cents-off stickers on all the day-old bread. My head still aches, and the smell of fresh bakery across the aisle makes me feel like puking. My hands smell like stale beer, which isn't helping. I hear the click of heels behind me, and when I turn around, there she is, staring at me.

Hello, she says. She's wearing a green dress, lots of make-up. Her hair is down, on her shoulders. I'm Julie Ann Thompson. Remember?

I don't say anything, but I stand up. With her high heels, she's almost as tall as I am.

I called and they told me you'd be here now, she says. You look handsome. She takes an envelope from her purse, and hands it to me. You forgot something.

I open the envelope. Two thousand dollars.

What's this? I ask.

It's yours, she says. You don't have to pay.

You're giving me the van, I say.

She nods. Yes, she says. Do you feel okay? She takes a step forward and reaches toward me, puts the cool palm of her hand to my forehead. I lean back and step away. I drop the money on the floor by her feet.

Can I hug you? she asks.

What for?

Just let me, please, she says, and reaches for me.

God damn, I say. I swear when I'm nervous. I'm like one of those skinny lizards who can swell his neck up to make himself look vicious.

The woman's face starts to twitch, like she's about to start crying again.

Is there a problem here? I turn around. It's Mr. Penfield. He always sneaks up on us to make sure we're working. Ma'am, can I help you with something? he asks.

No, she says.

He jerks a finger at me. Allan, can I see you for a minute in my office? I follow him, content, at least, to be escaping Mrs. Mountain Brook. We walk up the steps to his office, and once we're inside, he closes the door. He's wearing his usual white shirt—which is stretched over his bulbous belly—and red-and-white striped Winn-Dixie tie. One of the other stockers says if you look at his tie cross-eyed, it looks like a candy cane stuck in a big pile of snow.

Allan, he says, this is the last straw. Haircut or no haircut, I can't have you swearing at customers.

She's not a customer.

What is she, then?

She's some woman I know. She's stalking me.

His face twists into a smirk. For crying out loud, kid, he says. She's old enough to be your mother.

Just forget it, I tell him. Am I fired, or not?

He looks at me and sighs. He holds up one finger, then delivers the one-more-chance speech again. He gives me the rest of the day off.

Go home, he says. Try to get your life together. Don't think I don't know what you've been up to. You look like hell, kid. Get some sleep.

When I leave the office, Mrs. Thompson isn't anywhere in the store. But when I get outside, I see her car parked in the lot. She's sitting at the wheel. The engine's running.

She follows me all the way home. Pulls right behind me into the driveway.

I hope I didn't get you in any trouble, she says. We're standing behind my car.

Stay away from me, I tell her.

Please don't do this, she says. Please. I want to be your friend.

I don't want her to start crying, so I try to be calm. Look, I say, I'm sorry about your kid, okay? I really am. I realize I look like him and everything, but I'm not him. My name's Allan Berry. Allan. Berry.

But that's not who *I* see, she says.

I feel like screaming. I'm going in the house, I say, and if you're not gone in two minutes, I'm calling the cops.

Please, can't we just talk? Can I take you to breakfast or something?

I walk toward the house. My mother is standing at the window with the curtain pulled back, watching.

Please Allan, Mrs. Thompson yells. She starts crying again.

I open the door, go in, and close it. My mother smiles at me.

If that don't take the cake, she says. She interested in you?

It's not what you think, Ma.

She laughs. A bit perverted, if you ask me.

No one's asking, ma.

Ten minutes later, when I look outside, her car is gone.

That night, when Piranha calls, I tell him I'm staying home. It's his turn to have the van—my turn's tomorrow—and he's upset I don't want to ride with him. But I feel like shit. I fall asleep before eight o'clock, and I don't wake until morning. I don't hear Mom and Dick. I don't hear the telephone. I oversleep, too, but I don't care. My pot is gone, so in the morning I just lay and daydream, playing with my lighter, curling hairs on the back of my hand with the heat, thinking about my pathetic life.

My high school science teacher used to say that water always wants to be air. That air wants to be fire, and that fire wants to be water. That this fundamental circle, this cycle of molecular longing, as he called it, ran the universe. To help us see this, he made us stand up and push our desks to the sides of the classroom. He gave each of us a note card with WATER, AIR, or FIRE written on it, and made us close our eyes and walk around. Every time a WATER bumped into an AIR, they had to stand and wait for a FIRE. If AIR bumped into FIRE, they waited for WATER, and so on. Then all three traded cards and became something else. I remember this clearly, because Gloria was in that class, and it was the first time I touched her hand. We were FIRE and AIR.

The teacher's whole point was that each of these things could only be one thing at a time, but they were always a blink away from becoming something else.

I think a long time about Fisher. If life were a TV show, someone would send me a secret letter about now, telling me I'd been a twin and adopted, that two women showed up for us and drew straws, and the short straw got me. But now this secret letter person has discovered that someone later switched us in our cribs, that I really was the long straw all these years, and just didn't know it. The show would end in a courtroom drama, with both sides fighting over who gets me, like I'm the last cookie in the jar.

Allan? My door flies open. Mom walks in. All night, that goddamn phone's ringing, and you're in here passed out. You better do something about that woman. I stopped answering the phone. I just unplugged the goddamn thing.

When I get in my car to go to work, I find an envelope with $2,000 in it on my seat. It scares me at first, like it's a poisonous snake or something, but I toss it in the glove box and try to forget about it.

Mr. Penfield smiles at me when I walk into the store. Good morning, Allan, he says. You're late, but you look good. Combed your hair even, that's nice. Start in aisle five, please. Some soup left to be stocked.

All day, I feel wary. Every time I turn a corner, I expect Mrs. Thompson to be there. But she's not.

At the end of my shift, Piranha comes by to drop off the van. I leave my car in the lot and take him home, then take the van back to my house. It's Friday night. They want me to pick them up at eight o'clock, and they want to do a road trip to Florida. Wavy Dave's got a quarter barrel on ice in his garage that we can take, and Randy's supposedly got an ounce of Panama Red, guaranteed to make your brain buzz like a chain saw. I'm sure it's just homegrown touched up with food coloring, but Randy's not smart enough to notice that.

When I get home, Mrs. Thompson's white Audi is parked in the driveway. I touch the hood as I walk by and it's cool, so she's been here awhile. I find her sitting at the kitchen table with my mother, drinking coffee, both of them smoking cigarettes.

Hello Allan, they both say, almost at the same time.

I walk past them without saying anything.

Get your butt back here, my mom says, to my back. But I keep walking.

With my bedroom door open, I can hear them talking. Mrs. Thompson is telling the whole, sordid tale, though she's past the be-heading part. After the funeral, she says, crying. A mother's worst nightmare, my mother says. Finally, the hugs and goodbyes. Mrs. Thompson is leaving. She says something about having to get back to have supper with her husband. My mom laughs, though I don't know what's so funny about that. I wait until I hear Mrs. Thompson's car start up before I come out.

What did she want? I ask.

You were a rude bastard, Mom says. You couldn't sit down and visit for a minute?

No I couldn't. So what did she want?

We talked about what it's like being a mother, what it's like staying up all night worrying about your children when they come home at all hours.

Oh, give me a break.

Don't be a smart ass, Allan. I'm no June Cleaver around here, I know that, but don't tell me I don't worry about you. Don't even start with me on that. The least you can do is be nice to that woman, after what she's been through.

She creeps me out, I say. I don't want her coming around here anymore.

Mom says, I don't see your name on the mortgage. I invited her for lunch tomorrow.

What?

She wants to pay for your college tuition. Wouldn't that be nice?

I roll my eyes. I already told you I'm not going to college, I say.

Maybe you should, she answers. Maybe this is your chance.

What are you talking about? I say. Because I look like her dead kid I'm supposed to go to college? How much sense does that make?

Don't waste your life, honey, she says.

Now I'm pissed off. I turn and head for my room. Once inside, I slam the door closed and lock it. I frantically dig around in my dresser drawers, find a half a joint flattened under a sweater, open my window, and light up. I've got a pint of Old Crow hidden under the bed, too, and I take chugs of that while I hold the smoke in my lungs. The bourbon burns my eyes and throat, makes my lips numb. I put the headphones on then, crank up some Nirvana, try to get a grip on things while I float, stoned and tuned up, on my bed. Outside, the light starts to fade. Night comes on.

About quarter to eight, I grab my lighter and my wallet and start up the van. I back it out the driveway, turn toward town, head toward Wavy Dave's house to pick up Dave and the beer. But halfway there, I decide I can't do it. I'm not sure why, but I just can't take another pathetic night of doing nothing. I drive right past Dave's house—he's sitting on the curb smoking a cigarette and his jaw drops as I pass him. In the mirror, I see him stand up and start waving his arms overhead like he's the lone survivor of a plane crash trying to summon help, but this only makes me smile and drive faster. I've got an REM CD cranked on the stereo, the windows all down, and I head for I-65. I don't know where I'm going.

I drive north. To Tennessee, it turns out. Three hours going, three coming back. The sun drops over my left shoulder. I pass fields of cotton, tobacco, miles and miles of pine trees waving in the wind. In Tennessee, I stop to piss and fill up at a rest stop, buy a Mountain Dew to stay awake, then turn around and head back.

I'm going about 80 when I cross back into Alabama, past that big rocket they've got at the welcome center. The whole time, I've been trying to think about anything but Fisher and Mrs. Thompson, but I can't. I try driving with the radio on loud, on soft, off. Windows open. Closed. Going fast. Going slow. Nothing helps.

About two a.m., my eyes gritty, I see Birmingham again in the distance, a glow of light inside a bowl of hills. A lone plane falls toward the airport, red lights blinking. Trucks roar past me, their turbulence rocking the van. A light rain starts falling, just a mist really, enough to make the tires hiss on the steaming highway. I have the windows closed, and the wipers come on every ten seconds or so, to give me a clear view. But seeing the city ahead makes my stomach clench. Road trips usually make you feel better, more alive or something, but nothing's changed for me. I haven't gone anywhere. Instead of feeling better, I feel worse. I can't stop thinking about Fisher and his mother, and buying this stupid van. It's like these thoughts change the air pressure inside my head, fill it up so there's no room for anything else.

So I get off the freeway and head into Mountain Brook, where the roads curve through the woods like dark rivers. I go slowly, dim my lights, float quietly along. I feel kind of tired now. My neck's stiff from watching the road. When I see the Thompson's driveway, I cut the lights and coast in. I turn off the van and pull the keys from the ignition. Everything's quiet. Under the hood, the engine begins to ping as it cools.

I look up at the Thompson's house. All the windows are dark, but yard lights illuminate the driveway and front porch. The backyard glows, with nearly all the greenish light filtered up through the water in the swimming pool. The pool man must have left the underwater lights on. I stuff the money into my back pocket, and I'm just about to hop out for the hitch home, when something comes to me.

I don't know where it comes from, but it's there in my head. It's like the idea for a story that blooms in your brain while you're listening to music.

I put the key back in the ignition. My hands start shaking so I rub them on my legs to try to calm down. Even the muscles in my chest start to quiver. I start up the van, shift into drive, take my foot off the brake. Slowly, I pull up the driveway, then off onto the grass. I run over a hedge of azaleas, the branches crunching and snapping under the tires, then drive around the garage to the back yard.

Once in back, I drive around the pool carefully, weave through several trees, circle a white gazebo surrounded by rosebushes, and stop. The pool's now about sixty or seventy feet ahead of me. It is enclosed by a Century Fence, diamonds of woven steel mesh four feet high, which makes me nervous.

When I hit the gas, I panic a bit because the tires spin in the wet grass, but soon I feel the tug of traction, and the van is hurtling toward the swimming pool. I steer toward a point between two steel fence poles, glance briefly at the speedometer—it's hovering above twenty-five—and before I can look up again, the van slams into the fence.

The airbag explodes. Poof! Like a giant white flower, it blooms instantly from the steering wheel and forces itself, soft and hot, into my chest. Then it slowly deflates, folds itself softly around me. I am stopped short. My foot is on the brake. The van has run over the mesh of the fence, stretched it flat, but the bar once wired across the top has sheared off on only one side and is wedged under the windshield wipers. The van's windshield is cracked. The front bumper is five feet from the water. Lights come on upstairs in the house. A few dogs in the neighborhood start barking. Through the woods, I can see other house lights coming on.

Hurrying now, I back up, the fence screeching against the oil pan, in the wheel wells, until I'm free of it. I hop out to flatten what's left of the fence, pull off the top bar, so there's a clear path to the water. Then I back the van up to where I'd started the first time. I shift back into drive, put my foot on the brake, and open the door. When I jump out and close the door, the van lurches toward the pool on its own, idling faster than I can walk. It moves along the ruts in the yard, on track, rolls across the broken fence, over the concrete apron of the pool. When it gets to the water, the front end falls in. For a moment, the van teeters on the edge. I run behind it, thinking I'll have to push, but I don't. It drops in nose first, the bottom of the frame throwing sparks as it slides, screeching, along the edge of the concrete.

For just a moment, the van floats, a blue ice cube in a giant martini. The engine hisses and steams. Millions of bubbles boil from under the front end. Gradually, the sides go under, then the windows, the top. As the van settles to the bottom, water gushes over all four sides of the pool, across the concrete apron, over my feet, and into the grass.

The whole upstairs of the Thompson's house is bright now. All around me, dogs are howling and barking. I imagine Mountain Brook people in silk pajamas speed-dialing the police on their cell phones. Already in the distance, I can hear sirens wailing. I imagine men in monogrammed bathrobes pulling shiny .38s and .44s from locked desk drawers, sleepy-headed children pressing their faces to windows.

For a moment, I feel that old feeling, and I think about running. My heart's hammering inside me and I know I'm like the hub of a wheel with all the spokes heading like arrows in my direction. But I don't go anywhere. There's nowhere I can go. Instead, I suck in all the air I can and I walk out to the end of the diving board, over the water. I sit down, my feet dangling, my wet shoes just above the sur-face. I look down at the van. Magnified by the water, it looks huge. In the distance, I hear people's voices growing louder.

And then I look up at the house, and she's there.

Illuminated from the back, Mrs. Thompson is upstairs, standing in a bathrobe in her bedroom window. Her hair is down. Her arms are crossed, calmly. And the oddest thing is, I don't feel like running anywhere. She's watching me. Staring at me. Smiling. The way she's looking at me makes me feel swollen up inside, like someone's trying to open up a tent inside my ribs. I smile back at her, stand and take a bow. She laughs and waves at me, claps her hands, wipes her eyes. We just keep looking at one another.

Even as a squad car pulls into the Thompson's driveway, its red and blue lights flashing, I just keep looking up at this woman. I'm not thinking about getting arrested, or fined, or being late for work. All I'm thinking is this: That at least one time in his life, everyone should have someone look at him the way she's looking at me.

Non

custodial
Fatherhood

For eleven months after my divorce, I wasn't allowed to see my own
son. I was a danger to him, they said. A bad influence. A poor role
model. Sad thing was, my lawyer didn't even argue with them.
He said let's not pick a fight we can't win. Let's put down a foundation
to regain visitation rights. Steady work for six months. Sobriety for
nine. Limited visitation after that. I said I don't think I can stand not
seeing my kid for nine months. He said you're sleeping in the bed you
made, Richard. That's the best deal you're going to get here. I said
I'd like to trade that deal for whatever is behind door number two.
My lawyer, he had no sense of humor. He said, What the hell are you
talking about.

So I started showing up for work after that. I climbed up on the
wagon and took the ride out of the bottle, and now I got what I wanted
but I don't know what to do with it. My kid Robbie is eleven years old.
He stays with me every other weekend and lives with my X the rest
of the time. Every other Friday after work I sit in the driveway in my
truck with the heater running, waiting for the X or my boy to spot me
from what used to be my house. Then Robbie slouches out with his
backpack hanging from his shoulders and we leave. I usually ask him,

"How was your week?" or something like that, and he shrugs and looks out the window, or if he's in a talkative mood, he'll shrug and say, "Okay." Then we go to the McDonald's or Hardee's drive-through window to order supper, and my truck smells like french fries and roast beef sandwiches as we make the hour-long drive back to my apartment.

The kid can eat. Big Macs, Big Roast Beefs, Super-Size Fries and sodas, he can wolf it all down. Sometimes makes me wonder if the X is even feeding him at all on the money they take from my check every two weeks for child support. I don't mind losing the money. Hell, he's my kid and I want him to have nice things, decent clothes, you know. But this winter the X is wearing a brand new winter coat, full length with fake fur—I assume it's fake—around the collar. Sometimes life don't make sense is how I feel about it. But what the hell.

So I get to see Robbie now but to me it don't seem to be going so well. It's like I'm dancing with somebody who's got one leg shorter than the other. Herky-jerky. I think maybe it would help if my boy was with me more, but my lawyer says it's too early to try to change things. This is the best it'll be for awhile. So I see Robbie when I see him, which ain't much, though what I'd do with him the extra time I don't really know.

Mostly, when he's with me, he plays video games. He sits on the floor wired to his Playstation, holding some wired contraption shaped like a fat, gray bat with colored buttons all over it. His eyes are locked on the TV like he's been hypnotized. One time I said to him, "Robbie, why don't you read a book or something instead of playing this shit all day?" It was a Saturday afternoon and he'd been at it already for like six hours.

He shrugged and didn't take his eyes off the screen. "What should I read?"

He had me there. I hadn't read a book since high school. I asked, "Don't they give you books to read at school?"

"Yeah, but I read them there."

That's about as long a conversation as we'll have. It's as if there is something standing between us, a window shade that's down and lets in just a sliver of sunshine.

I'm a roofer, and in the winter, in Wisconsin, as you can imagine, things get a little slow. There's always plenty of work—the range of temperatures we get here beats the shit out of shingles—but at times with ice or snow coming down you can't go out to the job. And that's a problem for me. Because if I don't keep busy, the little genie in a bottle starts whispering in my ear. Idle hands make me thirsty, I guess. Anyway, couple years ago in late October, I woke up and it was snowing pretty hard—an early snow, even for this part of Wisconsin. The X was out of town for a few days. Her mother had fallen earlier in the week and broke her hip, and she had to fly down to Fort Lauderdale to be with her. We'd been fighting like raccoons all month so it was just as well. Consequently, I was home alone with Robbie on a Friday and I got him off to school okay. Then I went over to Eddie's—he's a guy I know, works in construction—and we ended up going to a bar to shoot some pool. From there we went back to Eddie's in the afternoon and one beer led to another. Three other guys came over and we played poker and drank all night. Eddie drove me home around midnight. I could hardly stand up. We pulled up the driveway and then I remembered, and it was like a shark closing its jaws over my heart: I forgot to pick Robbie up from school.

I panicked. I started shouting his name, I think, while I was still inside Eddie's car. My hands started shaking and I just kept thinking something must have happened to him because the house was dark. Eddie got me calmed down, and while I was puking in the bushes he found Robbie curled up in an old appliance box on the garage floor covered up with an old rug, his teeth chattering, trying to sleep. I had locked him out of the house.

Eddie got him inside and made him a couple of those toaster waffles that he found in the freezer, then got him into bed. Next morning the kid wouldn't talk to me, wouldn't even look at me. But this is the kind of kid my boy is: he didn't tell the X about it when she got home. She found out about it a couple days later when one of the nosy neighbors told her she saw Robbie trying to get into the house through a window on Friday night.

Even so, when I got served the divorce papers on the job, I felt like someone had swung a sledgehammer into my stomach. I had to come down off the roof to have my head handed to me, and I didn't go back home. I stayed with Eddie and got drunk five days in a row. I did other things I'm not going to talk about, things I'm ashamed of today. Called her on the phone at three in the morning cussing, things like that. But we're divorced now and in a ceasefire, and I get to see Robbie the equivalent of four days a month.

This Friday we don't have much conversation as we drive home, Robbie and me. It's mid-March, close to spring, but the dirty snow is still piled waist-high on the sides of the roads. We eat our food and I turn on the radio, some classic rock deal, and he looks out his window and drinks from his half-gallon Coke through a red, white, and blue-striped straw. Just before we get to the town where I live a deer runs from the woods up ahead on my left and crosses through our headlights to the other side of the road. Robbie sits up and points and says, "Look!" I hit my brakes and slow down, and then another one, a smaller one, a fawn from the previous summer, comes out, and I have to stop because she stands straddling the center line staring at us, her eyes shining like little flashlights.

"She's pretty, ain't she?" I say.

He nods and slurps from his now almost empty soda. The fawn clatters off into the darkness, and I accelerate towards home.

My apartment is a tiny two-bedroom place in a four-unit building, two downstairs and two—one of them mine—up. Refrigerator and gas stove furnished, laundry machines in the basement, all for five hundred a month, heat extra. It don't seem like a lot of money, but by the end of the month, especially in the winter, I'm tapped out. I've got an old plaid sofa and matching chair in the living room, which I picked up cheap at Goodwill, where I also found my kitchen table and chairs, one of those 1960s sets with a white Formica top and four padded chairs with metal frames, all of which have duct tape holding the stuffing in. I've got the TV sitting on a couple of cement blocks in one corner of the living room—a decent sized TV, twenty-five-inch screen—with a VCR wired in next to it on the floor. The carpeting throughout is a kind of dirty gray color, and on humid days it smells like the previous renters must have owned a cat or two. The kitchen and bedrooms are small, but the living room is decent sized, I guess, with windows facing south so I get some sun.

"You got homework?" I ask, as the boy drops his backpack. He takes off his coat and hangs it on a hook.

He nods. "It's not due until Monday."

"Well, why don't we do it now?"

He stares at me, puzzled. Homework is something his mother always kept track of, to tell the truth. Someone at my AA meetings told me if I take more of an interest in his school work, it might help me start building a bridge to the boy.

"What you looking at?" I ask.

"Mom helps me with my homework on Sunday night."

"Well maybe this time you and me could do it. Or maybe we could divide it up. What subjects do you have?"

"Just math," he says. "Three story problems."

"The new math or the old math?" I ask. I don't know what that means, exactly, but I once heard there's a new math out there.

He stares at me again. Then his mouth twists into a smile. "It's middle-aged math," he says.

I smile at him. "I'm middle-aged! Sounds perfect for me."

"Actually, it's called Every Day Math."

"Because you have math homework every day?"

He shakes his head, then says, "Well, sort of." He takes in a deep breath, picks up his backpack, and carries it to the kitchen table, me trailing him. He pulls a yellow pencil and a worksheet out of the backpack and sits down. I sit beside him, to his right.

"All right, let's see here," I say. I read the first problem aloud:

"Mary lives one hundred miles from her grandmother. She decides to take the train to visit. If the train goes fifty miles per hour for the first sixty miles and eighty miles per hour for the remaining forty miles, how long will it take the train to get to her grandmother's?"

Robbie looks at me, the eraser of his pencil held between his lips. He's a cute boy, looks like his mother. He's got black hair with enough curl to it that he can't really comb it, dark eyes, and a thick lower lip.

I exhale. "Jesus Christ, Robbie," I say. "Is this what kids are doing in the fifth grade these days?"

Robbie's pencil drops from his mouth. "Dad, I'm in sixth grade."

"Oh shit, sorry. That's right. I knew that."

He looks back down at the problem and I do, too. "Damn, Robbie, I just don't know. I mean, why would a train go fifty miles an hour for part of the trip and eighty miles an hour for the rest? It makes no sense. I've never heard of a train that did that."

"Maybe the conductor was drunk." He looks at me, smirks a bit.

I decide to let it pass.

"Nah," I tell him. "If the conductor was drunk, he'd be going a hundred miles an hour, and he'd drive that fucker right off the tracks."

Robbie chuckles. I stare at the problem again. "Shit, Robbie, maybe you should do this with your mom."

He shakes his head. "It's not that hard, Dad. Look." He writes some numbers in the white space under the problem, biting his lower lip while he does so. He has his left hand on his forehead, his elbow propped on the table. "Okay," he says. "It takes an hour and ten minutes to go the first sixty miles." He pauses. "And it takes just a half-hour to go the last forty miles. You don't even need to write that part down to figure it out. So you add an hour ten and thirty minutes and you get an hour and forty minutes. That's the answer."

"Wow," I tell him. "You're smart."

"Only in math," he says. "I suck at everything else."

"I doubt that," I say. "What's your teacher's name?"

"Why? You gonna to call her?"

"No. I just want to know."

"Mrs. Erdmann. Behind her back, kids call her 'Mrs. Turdman'."

"You too?"

He shrugs. "Sometimes."

"Is she nice?"

"She's okay." He looks back down at his math sheet. "Can I finish these Sunday at Mom's house?"

"Sure." He slides the paper into his backpack. "I can calculate the square footage of a roof," I feel compelled to tell him. "It's something that I have to do at my job, to figure out how many bundles of shingles I'll need. I've been doing roofs so long that I can look at a roof from the ground and tell you pretty much how many squares are up there, and how many bundles of shingles you're going to need."

He looks at me and nods.

"That's my every day math," I tell him. "Roofing's important work. If you have a hole in your roof, everything underneath it's going to get ruined."

He nods again, zips up his backpack, and slides off of his chair. "Can I go play Playstation?"

"Yeah sure."

Saturday passes the same way, him in front of the TV screen, playing something called Twisted Metal 3, blasting at cars with flame-throwers and missiles, and I drop him off at the X's on Sunday after supper and tell him I'll see him in two weeks. He smiles at me and walks around the front of my truck, up the sidewalk, and into the life of his mother, who's waiting for him inside the front porch. I watch him as long as I can. He takes off his coat, hangs his backpack up on a hook, and then wanders off the porch into the house. When the porch goes dark, I drive home alone.

⁂ ⁂ ⁂ ⁂ ⁂

I can't say I don't ever think about drinking because I do. I have been sober for 287 days, but it's not something I brag about or feel compelled to tell everyone. Some of the people who go to the meetings feel like they have to tell everybody everything. Every time they take a dump they announce it, and then they thank God for giving them the opportunity. There's a lot of bullshit at these meetings, but I have to do their 12-step tango to satisfy the arrangement that lets me see my boy. My sponsor is some guy in a wheelchair named Stan, who got that way because he blacked out and drove his Ford *Taurus* off the end of a cliff or something, like in that movie, *Thelma and Louise.* His car caught on fire and cooked him like a piece of bread in a toaster. Today, the skin on his arms and neck looks like melted cheese. Jesus. He's religious as hell now, too, which I guess you would be, going through something like that.

The meetings take place Monday nights in the basement of the Senior Center, just a few blocks from my apartment. There's about nine or ten people there most weeks, a couple women, the rest men, all sitting in a circle with snow melting off of our shoes, making little puddles on the tile floor. We bring our copies of AA's *Big Book*—the Big Kahuna, I call it—and we refer to it from time to time, though most often we just look at the 12 Steps, which, after the first couple, are mainly religious. I'm still hovering around step one, truth be known, which is to admit my life became unmanageable because I was powerless over alcohol. We go around and announce how many days it's been since we've had a drink, and everybody claps for everybody, and then people tell stories of shit they did that week, and how they're doing on the 12 Steps, that sort of thing. I don't usually talk much, but this Monday when the question goes out, "What changes would you like to see in your relationships with other people?" I raise my hand and say I'd like to see my son more than I see him now, which is just 96 hours a month. Four 24-hour days. I can do the math.

"How much do you want to see him?" someone asks.

"I don't know," I answer. "Maybe a couple days every week as well as every other weekend."

"How often did you see him before you were divorced?"

"Every day," I say. Lots of people nod and smile at me, sympathetically. But the discussion leader, a guy named Steve, who has a blonde ponytail and scruffy beard, wears Birkenstocks with wool socks, one of those save-the-world types, kicks in. He wears turquoise rings on several fingers of both hands, which seems weird to me. Most of the men I know don't have anything on their hands but calluses.

"How old is your son?" Steve asks.

"His name's Robbie," I say. "He's eleven. He'll be twelve soon."

"When?"

I scratch my head. "August. I think. In the summer, sometime."

Steve frowns. "What do you think it means that you don't know exactly when his birthday is?"

"It means I forgot." A couple people chuckle, but not Steve. He leans toward me and props his elbows on his knees.

"Why do you want to see him more?" he asks.

I shrug. "I don't know. I can't seem to get to know him right now."

"Maybe you feel a sense of urgency, a sense you need to make up for lost time?"

"Maybe," I answer.

"Were you part of his life, were you when you were drinking?" he asks. "Did you walk him to school, help him with homework, cook for him, take him to the library, things like that?"

"His mother did those things with him," I say. "I had to go to work. We did his homework together last Friday, though."

"Did your drinking ever hurt your son?"

I pause. "Yeah. It did," I say.

"How?"

"How the fuck should I know?" I say, loudly. Steve just watches me, doesn't respond. "Yeah all right, it did." I say the first thing that comes to mind. "Once on Christmas Eve, my X and I had a fight, and I knocked over the Christmas tree. Robbie started crying and ran up to his room. I sat there on the floor, throwing ornaments against the wall, watching them explode."

"Did your drinking ever put him in danger?"

I think, *Enough with all the fucking questions!* In the past I would have knocked this hippie's smug ass out of his chair. But now I think about an answer to his question. I tell everyone the story of how I forgot to pick Robbie up from school. Talking about it starts a little waterfall in the back of my throat, but I don't cry. I'm not that type.

"Have you ever apologized?" Steve asks. "Have you ever said 'Robbie, I'm really sorry for that afternoon I forgot to pick you up at school'?"

I shake my head no. "No," I say, frustrated, "But I'm making it up to him. Last Friday I did his homework with him."

Steve nods and smiles now. "That's what you said. And how did that go?"

"It was okay."

"And how did your son feel about it?"

I shrug. "I don't know. I guess he liked it all right."

"Good," Steve says, and gives a little nod. And then everybody claps and the big woman sitting next to me in this thick green winter coat that makes her look like a giant shrub pats me on the arm and smiles. Then we move on to someone else, some guy named Andrew who starts sobbing into his hands at least once every week. You want to tell him sometimes, "Buddy, suck it up. For Christ's sake, you're a man. Act like it." He always wears a nice suit and fancy wing-tips, so he looks like he's doing all right for himself. But of course the nice suit and shoes, that don't mean shit. On the inside, he probably feels like he's been in a train wreck, all twisted up and mangled. I don't know his full story, but I'm sure he'll get around to blubbering the gruesome details sooner or later. I admit that when I get to thinking about all the shit I put Robbie through, I feel like someone's taken an eggbeater to my guts, too.

✖　　✖　　✖　　✖　　✖

The next time I see Robbie it's an early April Friday night and we're getting one of those late spring blizzards, the kind where the snow is thick and wet and heavy and sticks to your shovel like snot when you try to get it off your sidewalk. Robbie comes out the door of his mother's house hunchbacked under his blue backpack, his eyes squinted against the blowing snow. The X walks out, too, that new winter coat over her shoulders, comes to my window and knocks on it.

I roll it down half way. "Nice coat," I say.

"It's snowing pretty hard out here," she says.

"Ain't so bad," I say, wondering where she's headed with this. "Plows are out. The roads are okay." Robbie climbs into my truck and closes the door. "Hey Robbie," I say.

He smiles at me.

"I don't know," the X says, crouching down to lean closer, like she's trying to smell my breath. "Do you think it's in Robbie's best interest to go out in this? There's a winter storm warning."

"I haven't seen the boy for two weeks," I tell her.

"I know that," she says, "but—"

"I can drive in the fucking snow," I tell her, my voice rising in anger.

"Watch your mouth," she says. "You think Robbie needs to hear that kind of language?"

An angry silence erupts. I roll up the window and shift into reverse. I hit the gas and the back wheels spin and throw slush, but then they catch and we race down the driveway to the road, the transmission whining. I shift into gear and jam on the accelerator and my tires spin and the truck slides a little bit left but straightens out. The X is standing there watching as we fishtail around the corner and head for the highway, wipers slapping at the snow.

I look over at Robbie and he's looking up at me.

"Little disagreement with your mother," I tell him. "So how was your week?"

"Okay," he says.

"Yeah? Good," I tell him. "Mine was okay, too. Listen, I've got an idea for us tonight. We'll eat, but then on the way home, we'll stop at the library to get some books."

Robbie frowns. "What for?"

"What do you mean, 'what for?' To read."

"Why?"

Man, the kid is demanding with all the questions. Maybe he'll be an AA discussion leader someday.

"Why?" I repeat. "Well, because it's supposed to be good for us, for one thing. It makes your brain bigger, or something."

"Does not," he says.

"Well, maybe it makes your dick bigger."

He laughs at this. "No way," he says. "I hate reading. I suck at it."

"Maybe you just need to practice," I tell him.

He looks out his window and crosses his arms, sulking. "I never see you reading a book," he says.

"You never seen me do a lot of things," I say.

He looks out his window, and I grip the steering wheel tightly, stare through the windshield at the snow coming at us like shooting stars through the darkness.

"I've seen you get drunk," Robbie says, suddenly.

This pisses me off, but I hold my tongue.

"Lots of times," he says.

"How long you going to keep bringing that shit up?" I shout. "What the fuck do you want me to say? I don't need you to be rubbing my face in it. Your mother can do that just fine without your fucking help."

Robbie doesn't answer. He turns his back to me, leans into the window.

Neither of us says anything more for many miles. The wipers pound back and forth and the heater fan hums under the dash, blowing hot air on our feet. The roads are slick, cars moving at a crawl.

"Look, I'm sorry," I tell him. "I shouldn't have shouted at you."
I take a breath, and plunge in with the rest. "Robbie, you know that
one day I forgot to pick you up from school and Eddie found you sleeping in the garage?" Robbie doesn't look at me but he moves his head
forward a little. His face is still against the window, the back of his head
to me. "I'm sorry for that," I tell him. "I was an idiot, okay? And I'm
sorry for all the other times I did shit like that. I fucked up a lot."

Robbie wipes his face with his hands. He's crying. "It's okay,"
he says.

"I'll make it up to you. Don't worry."

He sniffles and nods.

"What'll it be tonight, then?" I ask him, anxious to change the subject. "Macs or Hardees?"

He shrugs but doesn't say anything.

"Well then," I say. "Let's go all out. How about Burger King?"

Robbie turns to me. Tears are shiny scars on his face. "Okay,"
he says. I reach over and pat him on the leg with my hand.

"Dad," he says, weakly.

"What?"

"Mom says we might move to Florida."

"What?" I say, more loudly than I'd intended. "What the hell are
you talking about?"

"To be closer to Grandma. To help her get around and stuff."

"When did she say this?" I ask him. My hands start shaking,
and anger spills inside me like poison leaking from a bottle.

He sniffs. "I can't remember."

Beads of sweat sprout on my forehead, and I turn the heater
fan down. I want to turn around and go back, pound on my X's
door and tell her there's no fucking way she's moving to Florida with
my son. We drive in silence for some time, and I struggle to hold my-

self together.

"Well," I tell him, "I guess we'll cross that bridge when we come to it. You want to live in Florida?"

He shrugs.

"They got alligators down there," I tell him. "Sometimes they eat people's dogs."

"Really?"

I nod. "Sometimes. And there are hurricanes, and it's like 120 degrees out every day. But let's forget about Florida for now."

"A hundred twenty degrees?" Robbie asks.

I shrug. "Let's not talk about it anymore."

"Okay," he says. But I can't stop thinking about it. My guts are boiling.

The snow is still blowing and falling hard when we get to the library, flakes that look as big as dollar bills. We slog through eight inches in the parking lot and stomp our feet off inside.

"All right," I tell Robbie, slipping my gloves into my pockets. "Here we are. What kind of books do you like to read?"

"None," he says, "remember? I hate reading."

"Maybe there's a book here about video games," I say.

He laughs. "I don't think so. At school when they force us to read I pick these *Animorphs* books. They're chapter books about kids who morph into animals to fight evil."

"Well," I tell him, "get a couple of those. You'll have to find them, though. It's been a long time since I've been in a library."

"It's not that hard to find things," Robbie says. "You just type what you want, and the computer tells you where the books are."

He shows me how the computers work—and they do work, slick as shit—and we find our books and I get a library card and we check them out. It all takes less than an hour, and by the time we get back out to the car it's covered with two more inches of snow. But we make it to my apartment and we sit down with our books in the quiet to read. We can hear the wind blowing snow against the windows and the ticking of the clock on the wall. I've got one of those battery-operated deals where a different bird sings every hour. Eight o'clock is already past, the song sparrow. Nine o'clock is the belted kingfisher. My favorite's the cardinal. Midnight.

Robbie squirms in his chair. On the cover of his book is a picture of a boy transforming into a brown bear. I see him looking over at me, but I try to keep reading. Mine is a book called *Noncustodial Parenting for Fathers: A Handbook for Success*. It says one of the first things divorced fathers do is go out and buy their kids something, and it makes me think of how I went out and bought Robbie's video game the Thursday night before he was supposed to stay with me for the first time. I remember I was wondering what the hell I was going to do to keep the kid occupied for two days.

"This is weird," Robbie says, looking up from his book.

"What is?"

"This," he says. "It's too quiet. Can we put TV on or something?"

"If we have the TV on we'll want to watch it," I say. I look at the clock. "Ten more minutes, okay? When the kingfisher sings, you can stop reading and turn on the TV."

"Shit," Robbie says. He looks up at the clock, and then returns to his book.

Sunday night I drop Robbie back at the X's house, and later, back at home, after I'm sure Robbie's sleeping, I call her on the telephone.

"Hello?" she answers.

"What's this shit I hear about you planning a move to Florida?"

Dead silence on the other end. Then she says, "Have you been quizzing Robbie about my life?"

"Hell no," I tell her. "It's just something he said. I want to know if there's any truth to it."

"I don't want to talk about this. What I do with my life is my private business." And she hangs up.

I call her back.

"What?" she says.

"Don't take Robbie away from me," I say. "Please."

"For eleven years you haven't given him the time of day. And now you want me to disrupt our life for your sake? You are a real piece of work, Richard." The phone clicks dead on the other end. I call back again, but she doesn't answer, so I put my phone down and leave hers ringing. After a few minutes, I pick up and get a busy signal, so she's probably got it unplugged. I slam the receiver of my phone down so hard on the counter top that the earpiece snaps off. It looks like a dog bone bitten in half.

Monday morning I call my lawyer and tell his secretary I need to talk to him immediately. She wants to take the kid to Florida, I tell him. I'll never see the boy. Can she do that? Can she just up and move that far away with my son?

He tells me just to stay calm and wait to see what happens. She can't do anything without notifying the court.

"I'm just getting to know the kid, for Christ's sake," I tell him.

"There's a process she has to follow if she wants to leave the state. She hasn't done anything yet. Maybe your son just heard her thinking out loud. You know how kids can twist things."

"I won't allow her to do this."

"Try to relax," he says. "Don't do anything you'll regret. You don't want to jeopardize the custody order you've got now. It isn't great, I know. But don't do anything crazy."

I'm still upset when the time comes for my Monday night meeting.

I'm sitting in my usual place in the circle and I feel like my stomach is full of bees, stinging me. I want to talk about this, but five minutes into the meeting Andrew shows up so drunk he's actually pissed his pants and can't even tell. The front of his gray slacks are dark and wet, and he's got an ugly gash above one eye from where he must have fallen down somewhere. Dried blood is crusted in the middle of his eyebrow, which makes it look like one of those woolly worm caterpillars. Andrew's shouting that he's going to kill himself, that he's going to blow his brains out with a gun. Jesus, he makes a scene. He's so loud that someone upstairs, one of the elderly ladies playing Bingo, calls the police, and in minutes two of them in uniform come downstairs to talk to Steve, who explains the situation. Andrew's sitting on the floor in one corner of the room with his legs crossed, blubbering, and then of course he vomits, sprays his muddy shoes and pants while everyone looks away. Eventually Steve contacts social services to come for Andrew, then he calls the meeting short and sends us home. On the way up the stairs, someone from the group tells me that nine months ago Andrew drove drunk with his four-year-old daughter in the car and got into a traffic accident that left the little girl paralyzed from the neck down.

On the job a few days later, they call me down off the roof just before lunch time. There's a guy in a suit who wants to see me. Fucker hands me an envelope and gets back into his car, drives away. The envelope is from the County, Family Court. I tear it open. The X has announced her intent to move to Florida with my boy by the end of the summer.

I get into my truck and hold my hands against my thighs to keep them from shaking. I am so filled with anger I have a hard time drawing breath. Eddie sees me and knocks on the window. I open it.

"What's up?" Eddie asks.

"My fucking ex-wife is moving to Florida with Robbie."

"Oh, shit. I'm sorry."

"I can't fucking believe this is happening."

But Eddie just shrugs. "So move to Florida too," he says. "Helluva a lot nicer down there. You could work all year long, make a ton of money."

"Too fucking hot," I tell him. "You ever been up on a roof when it's a hundred degrees? Feels like you're standing barefoot in hell's waiting room. No way I'm getting fried to a crisp everyday just to make a living. Besides, I'm not following her around the country like some goddamn puppy." I look him in the eye. "Maybe I should just take Robbie and move somewhere myself. I could set up a roofing business, put some ads in the paper. I could get Robbie enrolled in school eventually and the two of us could live together."

"What do you mean, like you'd kidnap the kid or something?"

"It's not kidnapping if it's your own kid, for Christ's sake."

"The hell it's not," he says.

"What you talking about?"

"Cops would be all over your ass before you could wipe it," Eddie says. "And even if you did manage it, how are you going to care for him? You going to feed him McDonalds and Kentucky Fried Chicken every day, morning, noon, and night? What are you going to do when he gets sick? What are you going to tell him when he asks about his mother?"

"He's my kid, too," I say.

"That's fucked up," Eddie says.

"I can't let her just take him away from me."

"Yeah, but what you're talking about," Eddie says. "It ain't right." He walks away shaking his head. I roll the window back up.

"Well fuck you, too," I tell him, though he can't hear me.

The rest of the week and through the weekend and through Monday, when I skip the AA meeting, I'm haunted. I just keep thinking of the years I missed out on Robbie, all my fault, I'll grant that, but now if the X moves to Florida I'll miss out on the rest of his childhood and maybe the rest of his life. Why should you be made to pay a lifetime for a decade of screwing up? That don't seem fair to me.

All this worry has got my insides cooking. I grab my keys a couple times with the intention of going down the road to the Kwik Trip. A few beers, I tell myself. That's all. Just something to take this damn edge off. She's driving me back to it, I'm thinking, just like she drove me to it all over those years with her yelling and her silent anger and her expectations. But that's bullshit. I know it. Much as we didn't get along, I know that part of it isn't her fault. I was drinking before I even met her. Hell, I was drinking even before I learned to crawl. My mama rubbed whiskey on my gums to keep me quiet when I was teething. Gave me an early taste of the good life.

Then the phone rings and it's Stan, my guardian angel. Not even twenty-four hours since I missed the meeting and here he is, tapping on my shoulder.

"Steve called and told me you missed the meeting yesterday," he says. "I'm just checking to make sure everything is all right." His voice is gruff, the sound of coarse sandpaper on metal. I think he even burned the inside of his throat when he had his accident.

"Everything's fine."

He's quiet for a few seconds. "I don't think so. If everything was fine you would have been at the meeting last night."

"Yeah, well, I didn't feel like going."

"So what's the problem?"

I think about this. "The problem is my ex-wife is being a pain in the ass and I don't know if there's anything I can do about it."

"You want to come over and talk about it?"

"Not necessary," I tell him.

"You sure?"

"I'm sure."

And so we hang up and I'm alone again. Fuck it. I throw on my coat and grab my keys, and pretty soon I've got a cold twelve-pack of Bud on the floor next to my chair. I sit up all night, one can after another, looking at a United States atlas, looking at a map of Michigan, thinking about possibilities.

✖   ✖   ✖   ✖   ✖

May comes and all the snow finally melts and the world is full of singing birds. Everybody wants their roof fixed yesterday. When I pick Robbie up on Friday afternoon, a bit earlier than usual, the X doesn't come out. She knows I got the papers about her little Florida caper, I'm sure. Robbie's got his backpack slung over one shoulder. He waves to me and runs to the truck, opens the door, climbs in.

"Hey Robbie " I say. "How you doing?"

"Great," he says. He pulls a piece of paper from his pocket. "Got my report card today. Third quarter."

He hands it to me and I open it up. "An A in math and Science," I read aloud. "Wow! B in Social Studies. B minus in Art. B in Gym. C in Language Arts." I smile. "Wow. Robbie, this is excellent."

He beams.

"Well hell, we have to celebrate!" I announce. "And just by coincidence I have a little something special planned, too. You and me are going to take a little trip. We're going to go down to Milwaukee. We'll stay in a hotel tonight, and then tomorrow night, we'll get up, and we'll go to the museum."

"The museum?" he looks at me, his eyebrows dropped into a frown.

"Hell yes. And if we get bored out of our socks, we'll go to the zoo, okay? They've got animals there from all over the world—monkeys, elephants, lions, tigers. You name it, they got it."

Robbie shrugs and smiles. "Okay," he says.

It takes us three hours to get down to Milwaukee. It's just for the weekend, just me and Robbie alone, out of our usual element. We don't play the radio, we talk. We talk some more about Robbie's report card, and I tell him some about the roof of the house I'm working on, pitched at sixty degrees to shed snow more easily in the winter. It's so steep, I tell him, I feel like Spiderman climbing up a building when I'm up there.

"You should charge them extra," he says, "for danger." He tells me about playing basketball on the playground with the other kids, about being a reading buddy to some kid in the second grade, and how they read aloud when the teacher is near by, but talk about video games together the rest of the time.

About forty-five minutes outside of Milwaukee, we pull off of the freeway to the parking lot of a family restaurant that advertises an all-you-can-eat buffet. Both of us are starving, and we load our plates up—chicken drumsticks, hot rolls, mashed potatoes and gravy, pork chops, french fries, brownies, cheesecake, sweet corn—we carry our plates heaped over to the table, devour everything, then go back for more. Robbie gorges himself. He eats like he hasn't eaten for weeks, laughing, going back for thirds and fourths, as he calls them, on dessert. He goes to the ice cream bar and makes himself a sundae as big as a softball with chocolate syrup and nuts and colored sprinkles all over it. And all the while I'm thinking that this boy is the most amazing thing. For so many years his life was a distraction to mine, a pull upon my time and energy. Now he's all I can think about. How could I have missed it.

"Dad," he says, "I got a joke for you."

"I'm listening," I tell him.

"Waiter," he says. "What's this fly doing in my soup? The waiter comes over and looks at it, then he says, 'It looks like he's doing the back stroke, sir'."

I chuckle. "That's a good one."

Throughout the meal, he tells me a half-dozen more. I sit and eat and watch my son tell jokes, and I can't stop smiling at him.

By the time we check into our hotel, a Holiday Inn on the west side of the city, it is nearly ten o'clock. We watch a bit of the ten o'clock news, and then Robbie gets ready for bed. There are two full-sized beds. Robbie chooses the one closest to the windows. We're on the fourth floor, and we have a good view of the interstate down below. He presses his face to the glass for a while, then lays down. Our room features one of those small, brown refrigerators stocked with snacks, cans of soda and beer, and little bottles of brandy, whiskey, gin, and vodka. I offer Robbie a bag of chips before bed, but he declines.

"My stomach hurts," he says.

"You feeling sick?"

He nods.

"You probably ate too much," I tell him. "After you sleep for awhile, you'll be okay." I tuck him in and after some tossing he drifts off to sleep. I watch a bit of Jay Leno's monolog, then hit the remote, turn out the lights, and close my eyes. In my mind, I can see the cans of beer lined up inside the refrigerator like old soldiers in a Veterans Day parade. I'm on the wagon again, 18 days now, but it doesn't seem to be getting any easier.

I awaken to the sounds of Robbie moaning and choking. I scramble to turn on the light, and in the brightness I find Robbie on his hands and knees in bed, vomiting violently into his pillow. Vomit is splashed down the front of his t-shirt, on the back of his hands, all over the bed.

His breathing is loud and raspy. His sides heave. Each time he takes in air, it's like he's sucking it through a straw. The room smells like old milk curdled and soured in the bottom of the carton.

"Robbie!" I say. "What's the matter?"

His back arches, he gags, and a plume of water pours from his open mouth to the bed.

"I can't breathe very good," he says, through tears. And then he wretches again and vomit, brown and watery, splashes against the pillow.

I get up and stand by his bed. It's nearly two in the morning. "Try to get to the bathroom so you can throw up in the toilet. It's a lot easier." I touch his shoulder gently. Gamely, he slides to the edge of the bed and puts a foot on the floor. He grabs my hand in his, slippery and wet and soured, and I put my other arm around his thin back. His chest quakes and rattles each time he sucks in a breath. We make about four steps and his body jumps as if someone had just kicked him in the stomach, and he sprays vomit on the floor and on our feet.

"Jesus," I say. "Come on Robbie. Just a bit further. You're doing great."

"I want Mom," he says, through tears. This stings slightly, and I ignore the request at first.

I flip on the light in the bathroom and Robbie drops to his knees in front of the toilet. He seems to be dizzy. His hair is wet with sweat, and his skin is clammy and pale. He's sitting back on his heels, his chin resting against the bowl, eyes closed. The rattle in his throat sounds like melt water dripping into a rain gutter.

"Are you okay?" I ask him. He doesn't move or speak. I sit on the edge of the bathtub, wipe my feet clean with a towel. He opens his mouth, gags and coughs, leans over the toilet bowl, then rests. His chest heaves.

"I want to call Mom," he says.

"Sure," I tell him. "It's awful early in the morning, though. Do you think you could wait a few hours?"

He shakes his head vigorously, pinches his watery eyes closed. "Now," he says. "I want Mom."

"All right," I tell him, getting up from the bathtub. "I'll call her. You just rest here for a minute."

I dial the number. After five or six rings, she picks up, sounding dazed.

"Hey, it's me," I tell her.

"Rick?" she asks. "What time is it?"

"Robbie's sick," I tell her. "He wants to talk to you."

"What's the matter with him?"

"He's throwing up," I tell her. "We ate at a buffet tonight and I think he had too much to eat."

"Did he eat any shellfish? Any shrimp or lobster, anything like that?"

"I don't think so."

"He's allergic to shellfish, remember? For Christ's sake, Rick." Her voice rises with panic. "Did he eat any shellfish or not? Shrimp, clam strips?"

I don't say anything. I want to ask when we'd learned he was allergic to shellfish, but I don't. I can't believe I don't know that. I panic. It's as if her desperation has passed through the phone line to me.

"Let me talk to him," she snaps.

"Hang on."

I go to the bathroom and find Robbie on his side on the floor. His eyes are closed. His face and lips look blue. "Robbie " I shout at him. He doesn't move. I drop to the floor and squeeze his face between my hands. "Robbie " I shout again. "Come on, man. Wake up."

He doesn't seem to be breathing. I run back to the telephone and hang it up without talking. Then I pick up the receiver and scream into it, scream at the desk clerk to call an ambulance, scream my room number over and over. I run back into the bathroom and roll Robbie to his back. I have no idea what I'm doing, but I tip his neck back, open his mouth, cover his mouth with mine, and blow air into him. My breath pours out his nose. I can feel it against my cheek. His mouth is warm and wet with vomit and stomach acid, and the sour smell and taste make me gag. Robbie doesn't move. I suck in another breath, pinch his nose closed, and breathe into him again. It's like blowing into a stiff balloon. In a panic, I roll him to his stomach and pound against his back. I hit him hard between his shoulder blades, and he lurches and coughs, vomits again, thickly, but then starts to breathe. I feel like shouting for joy. I watch him closely, bend over him, my face just inches from his. He pulls a knee up underneath himself, moans, and breathes again, mouth open. Slowly, the blue in his lips begins to fade. I sit down next to him, rub my fingers against his back, close my eyes.

Ten minutes later I hear fumbling at the door and then two paramedics, a man and a woman, burst in carrying a suitcase, with the night manager standing behind them. By now, Robbie is sitting up on the bathroom floor, sipping water from a glass, rinsing his mouth out and spitting into the toilet.

"He's okay," I tell them. "He was choking. He seems to be doing all right."

"You feel all right?" they ask him.

He nods at them and smiles. "I think I ate too many desserts." The paramedics check him over, they listen to his heart, take his blood pressure, look into his eyes, nose, and mouth, check his pulse rate. He seems to be fine, they tell me. He probably aspirated something, they say, which temporarily blocked the airway. Do I want them to take him to a hospital? A doctor might put him on antibiotics as a precaution against pneumonia. He might have aspirated something into his lungs.

Robbie shakes his head. He doesn't want to go.

No, I tell them. I think he's going to be all right.

I call the X back to tell her everything is okay, that Robbie choked a bit, but that he's all right now. My hands have not stopped shaking, but my voice is no longer quivering.

"I'm coming over," she says.

"We're not at my place," I tell her. "We're at a Holiday Inn on the west side of Milwaukee, just off Silver Spring. We're going to the museum tomorrow morning."

Silence on the other end. "The museum," she says, flatly.

"That's right."

"Does he have a fever? Was there any blood? Does he have a sore throat?"

"No, he's fine. We had supper at an all-you-can-eat place and he had more than he could eat and then some. He didn't eat any shrimp. He knows he's allergic. He had three pieces of cheese cake, two brownies, and a big bowl of ice cream for dessert alone."

"Don't just take it lightly and assume it's nothing," she says. "It could be strep throat. He could have the flu."

"Hell, he could have cholera, Sharon, but he doesn't. Look, he's falling asleep on my bed right now. The paramedics checked him out and he's fine. He looks great. The room's a fucking mess, but Robbie is doing fine."

"I'd feel more comfortable if I could see him."

"And I'd feel more comfortable if you'd stop treating me like a child."

Sharon sighs into the phone.

I tell her, "Don't worry about it. I can take care of him."

I clean up Robbie's bed. I put his pillows and blankets inside the comforter, roll it up, and set it against the wall on the far side of the room. With a wet bathroom towel I wipe up the spot where he'd spit up on the floor. I wipe off the toilet and bathroom floor with wads of toilet paper and flush the bowl clean.

When I finish cleaning the room, I sit on the other side of my bed and turn on the TV awhile, watch "CNN Headline News" and then a bit of The Weather Channel. Robbie breathes deeply beside me, still curled into a ball. I look at Robbie and for no reason at all, none that I can identify clearly, I start to cry. My chest starts heaving and the tears flood my eyes. It embarrasses me. I turn away from Robbie and grab a handful of tissues from the nightstand, jab at my eyes with them. Then I turn off the lights in case Robbie still isn't completely asleep. I hold the tissues in my fisted hands, and I lie down next to him, put an arm lightly over his chest, and wet my pillow like a baby.

The ringing telephone wakes both of us at eight o'clock. Sun pours through the windows. I answer.

"Telephone call for you, sir," a girl's voice says. And before I can say anything I hear the X's voice. "Hello?" she says.

"Sharon?"

"How's Robbie?"

I look at him. He squints his eyes, stretches and yawns, then smiles at me. "He's fine," I tell her. "He's doing fine. You don't have to worry." I can hear the hum of traffic on the interstate down below.

She says, "I'm down in the lobby."

"What in the hell are you doing?"

"I'm sorry," she says. "I was worried. I need to see him. Is he still sleeping?"

"He was until the damn phone rang."

"Who is it?" Robbie asks, sitting up.

"It's your mother," I tell him. "You want to see her? She's down in the lobby." He nods happily.

"All right," I tell her, running a hand through my greasy hair. "Come on up. We're in 436."

After an awkward breakfast together in the hotel restaurant, where we said every possible thing that could be said about the fish tank on display full of goldfish so fat they looked like they had all swallowed golf balls, goldfish with dark strings of poop trailing behind them—a fine thing to have in a restaurant—Sharon decides to follow us to the Milwaukee Public Museum in her Subaru. Robbie's idea. At breakfast, during one of the lulls in the goldfish conversation, he has a brainstorm and invites her to come along with us. Sharon looks at me and she says she might just do that. We look at each other but don't say anything. I shrug my shoulders as if to say what the hell, why not, but I'm hoping she won't come along. Now I watch her car behind us in my rear view mirror as Robbie and I make the short drive downtown.

I find a parking place around the corner from the museum, but when we get out of my truck, Sharon pulls up beside us and opens her window, tells us she's really tired and has a lot of work to do back at home. I feel relieved. Robbie kisses her through the window and we both wave as we watch her drive away. Then Robbie and I cross the street, turn the corner, join the line of people at the glass doors.

It strikes me that I can't remember actually ever being inside a museum. It is filled with things, magnificent old things, I have never seen. Robbie gapes in open-eyed wonder at everything. He reads aloud from the posted explanations that accompany each display. Though we didn't intend to, we pass the entire day in just one wing of the museum, touring the Paleozoic, Mesozoic, and Cenozoic eras, cases upon cases of beautiful rocks and minerals, meteorites, rooms full of the skeletons of large and small dinosaurs, mastodons, saber-toothed tigers.

"Awesome!" Robbie says, again and again.

The day passes. It's exhausting, but we cannot seem to get enough. Near closing time we find ourselves standing on a balcony in a large room, enthralled by a life-sized, three-dimensional tableau of an ancient landscape, where a towering Tyrannosaurus Rex, its head in the shadows near the ceiling, has killed and started to eat a Triceratops, which lies in the muck on its side, its open eyes glassy and gray in death, its colorful offal already pouring from a gaping wound in its stomach. My throat is dry from breathing museum air all day, and my legs are heavy from walking, but this scene fills me with energy. Loudspeakers hidden in the room offer the hushed sounds of extinct, exotic birds, which fade and then return at regular intervals. An artificial sun rises and sets on this scene, the light growing and fading, over and over, days and nights passing in a matter of seconds. Each time the sun rises, I look down at Robbie, and his bright face glows. We stand this way in the rising and falling light until we're the only ones left in the room. An usher in a red sport coat comes into the room, glances up at us, and motions us toward the door. "Closing time," he says. We pretend not to notice him. I stand watching with Robbie, his small, sweaty hand in mine.

Acknowledgments

Thank you to the following publications, where several of these stories first appeared: "Crop Dusting" appeared in *Orchid, A Literary Review* (Volume 3, Spring, 2004). "Instructional Technologies" was first published in *The Talking of Hands* (New Rivers Press, 1998). "Like Water Becoming Air" first appeared in *Fox Cry Review* (Volume 28, 2002).

I feel such a profound personal and professional debt to so many people that these few words of acknowledgement are not nearly enough. Thank you to Mark Friere and the Wisconsin Arts Board for the literary arts fellowship that supported the completion of several of the stories in this collection, and to the University of Wisconsin Oshkosh, which awarded me the John E. Kerrigan Endowed Professorship in 2001, an endowment that provided, among other things, the much-needed computer upon which these stories were composed.

Thanks also to the talented people at the new, New Rivers Press, for your encouragement, your commitment, and the marvelous work you've done on this book.

My creative writing students and my kind friends and colleagues in the Department of English and the COLS Dean's Office are in these pages in spirit. I'm especially grateful to Michael, Diane, and Barb; Jane, Sandy, Pam, P.K., Charlie, Jordan, Margaret, Roberta, Paul, Doug, and Estella for years of intellectual vitality, laughter, and good will. Thanks also to my Ripon College friends: David G., Kate, and David S., the last of whom catches many more trout than I do when we're out on the river during the Hex hatch.

Thank you Fred Ashe, my Alabama brother, for years of dazzling correspondence and unbridled vitality. Roll Tide.

Though they sometimes seem uncertain about my calling and the path it has taken me, my parents and siblings have remained supportive and loving always—thanks to all of you for that constancy.

My wondrous children and stepchildren are a gift I hope I never take for granted. Thank you Della, Claire, Tyler, Riley, and Noah for the noisy, full life you give back to me.

And finally, I will never be good enough with words to adequately thank my wife, Jenna, for giving me the title of this collection, and for lighting my body, soul, and spirit on fire. As Eudora Welty wrote, the time people come into our lives makes a difference. Love is a force, Sweet Girl.

A Midwesterner since birth, **Ron Rindo**
lives with his wife and five children on a small hobby farm in Pickett,
Wisconsin, where they raise bantam chickens and grow fruit trees
and organic vegetables. His published work includes two story collec-
tions, *Secrets Men Keep* (1995) and *Suburban Metaphysics and Other Stories*
(1990), both of which were named outstanding books of the year by
the Wisconsin Library Association. His work has received many
other grants and awards, including several Pushcart nominations and
a 2003 artist's fellowship from the Wisconsin Arts Board. He teaches
English at the University of Wisconsin in Oshkosh.